D1608186

COUNTRY PEOPLE

By Larry Schnell

In a small town in rural New York, in the wooded hills between Cooperstown and the Mohawk Valley, those who socialize can have no preferences. The poor mingle with the rich and educated. Laborers rub elbows with teachers. Drunks socialize with respectable residents, and sinners share their lives with churchgoers.

ACKNOWLEDGMENTS

For my parents, Arthur and Florence Schnell, a couple city people who found beauty in rural New York.

Cover photo illustration by Larry Schnell
I wish to thank Bill Schnell for the use of his cabin for the cover design. I am grateful to Zoe and Pebbles for their appearance in the cover photograph.
Thanks to Debra Donahue for editing.

The first six stories are works of fiction. The characters, names, places, and events depicted in them are fictitious. The final story, *Dad's Dump*, bears striking resemblance to my family members and events.

TABLE OF CONTENTS

LAURA

I am going to tell the story as I heard it, or one way that I heard it, for stories have a way (among ignorant folk) of changing as a river changes as it flows along, sometimes overflowing its banks, sometimes meandering from one spring to the next, never taking the same course twice. This story certainly overflowed its banks and the banks of credibility as well, but no one seemed at all bothered by flooding in the valley of ignorance. No, instead the people of Bloomville washed their feet in that ubiquitous nonsense and suckled their children on the same muddy water.

My mind strays easily. Again, the story. It seems to start first with another story, and I will attempt to accurately reproduce the two, interjecting comments only when I feel I must compensate for the basic ignorance of my story tellers.

Old Darwin Sickler was a peaceful enough fellow, living in a cabin with his wife, Elsie, and their four children. He was a portly frog of a man, she a lively wench, the children like the parents normal and healthy. Who would have thought it, Darwin being a churchgoer, that one bright day in April, the old man went as berserk as

Elwin Tillman's old hound (Elwin is a neighbor of mine who will turn up later) and shot them all in cold blood.

When Evelyn Allen stopped in that evening with some loaves of fresh, warm bread, she saw the five dead and old Dar sitting on the porch peacefully smoking his pipe, staring off somewhere in apparent contentment. He was shortly taken to the Justice of the Peace, who knew he should arrange a trial, but at the same time he had to listen to the lynch mob outside, not the quietist of whom was the good Reverend of the Methodist Church. The Justice of the Peace did what most men do when they cannot make up their minds. He appointed a committee. It was headed by the Reverend, a good organizer if nothing else, and they solved the entire dilemma in a matter of minutes by locating a length of sturdy rope, which seemed acceptable to everyone. Darwin was clearly in a bind when studying the fine manila strands he could not find so much as one flaw and so had to agree with the findings of the committee, thereby absolving them of all responsibilities. He was quiescent on that fatal morning when he stepped onto the scaffold. Before departing, the old fool repented saying, "Forgive me for I know not what I done." With that they pushed him off. He danced a bit, shivered a little and then relaxed.

The people who bought his old shack in the woods a few months later said they could not use the water from the well because the blood from Darwin's family ran down it (it was next to the house) and ever after it pumped red water.

This red water theme is easy to ridicule but it is a type I've run across frequently. It seems to be related to man's need to have tangible remnants of the past living with him in the present as a memorial or some such symbol. And he needs these remnants most where great acts of violence, love, or death have occurred. It is not unrelated to the gravestone tradition as I see it. (For a complete study of the subject, see *The Living Stone* by F. Norton Hamilton.)

About a month after Darwin died, a story began to circulate that he wandered through the woods and fields and valleys with a lantern, which he swung gently, weirdly from side to side as he sought his missing head. One can see for example why scholars of ancient Irish lore curse their ancestral scribes—foolish monks—when the adventitious figure of Christ appears in the scene set somewhere in the B.C.s. Christ is next to integral when compared to the headless Darwin, who makes even myself, a professional story collector, cringe at the nonsense these people will permit to pass their lips. A man without a head needs no lantern to find it for he has no eyes, which are of course the light-sensitive receptors of our being; and he may as well have walked in utter darkness, undoubtedly the very same through which his ilk in town grope. Besides, no one who witnessed the hanging recalls the head separating from the body.

But like the scholars of ancient Irish lore, I must concentrate on the few fragmented facts that remain. There is more.

A girl named Laura Pierce lived in the hill country south of Bloomville in a fine, large house that she later inherited from her industrious though not wealthy and of course now dead parents. She was born in Bloomville. She grew up there. She was the belle of the town, a classic picture of immature beauty at twelve, a truly stunning woman at twenty-one. She was beloved by the town for she reveled in altruistic deeds. She visited people in their illnesses and gave small amounts of money and candy to poor and hungry urchins who followed her about the sidewalks and parks like a herd of animals. Her virtue seemed limited only by her frailty—her small, thin but shapely frame, which made her parents somewhat overprotective. She was not allowed to participate in as many "goodwill" activities as she would have desired.

It was her good nature that precipitated her early end (they said in Bloomville), but her reward is in heaven (that catchall where those unsuccessful in life have their just due—my note). She frequently walked the rough miles between her home and Bloomville in order to spend some time with Mrs. Miller, who lost the use of her legs. Laura helped her dress, bathe, cook, sew and assisted her in other niceties which nature would have correctly deprived the old woman of (along with her miserable life) had it been allowed to take its proper course.

But through the help of friends and the life-sustaining breath of the Holy Spirit, the woman dangled by that golden chain until one of its lightly plated links gave way. I am getting ahead of myself. Laura walked the rough miles alone. She visited the place about three times a week. She began the walk about dusk, not returning home until midnight or later, when weary from the long and perhaps frightening jaunt, she would tiptoe up the stairs, crawl quietly into bed, falling asleep almost immediately.

Why did she walk alone? Indeed, should she have walked alone? The natives frequently asked these questions, having nothing better to concern themselves with. After all, the rough, rolling countryside was plagued with dangers for a frail girl. Most, through some erroneous reasoning, answered the questions simply by laying the blame on the husband, a bright, well-educated though somewhat aloof fellow and a rather attractive man who snatched the lovely creature from the faithful fold, selfishly depriving her of her precious virginity sometime before the grand occasion of the sacred rites. Actually he found little difficulty because she was really a very lonely girl, and he had first to make her see her loneliness and then instruct in the paradoxical ways of nature—the loneliness, the love, the cruelty, the kindness, the beauty, the horror—and she melted like so many candles consumed by their own flames.

To bring the story to a rapid conclusion, one dark night, wisps of mist wandering in ghostly aimlessness through the black trunks of trees (damn them and their love of the gothic—it was a clear night, the moon shining fair) she walked back home and saw the lantern gently waving, its yellow light breaking through the woods in shafts. She stopped but did not scream or panic. She must have felt the malignity, or at least the cold indifference of the woods, as barren as a bleak winter sky. But she had, as a crusader who has been given some divine promise of security, a degree of composure as she watched the light move closer. Yes, Darwin Sickler, the headless man. She must have been certain of it as the light approached, for it had been seen three times now, and I'm sure the story would have reached her quickly.

Laura watched until the light was so close that she could make out the form behind the yellow sheen of lantern light. It was the dark shape of a man, except it had no head.

She turned, ran, and at the same time heard the lantern fall and shatter. She must have felt lost and helpless, stumbling in the utter darkness, where the dimensions of time and space drew in their eternal boundaries, condensed themselves into one great act of frantic escape. She had the lead at first, which must have given her a false sense of optimism, which in turn must have made the capture that much more of a blow, a cruel reality breaking through her feeble illusions. When she heard the heavy breathing, the footsteps close at hand, she must have come near despair. There was no hope. Nature's frailty could not compete with the brute force of the universe. In a second she was thrown off balance and lay helplessly on the ground, where the dark shadow, like a bird of prey, brutally and painfully ravished her thin body on dew-wet grass, choked the life blood from her feeble frame, and her blood drained tranquilly onto the ground.

In a second the effort was over, the night slept again, closing its eye with weary indifference on the scene. The dew continued to fall uninterrupted on trees, grass, stream, and corpse alike.

It will be readily evident to the astute reader that this is not the correct version of the story. True, all the events except the murder may be verified by one or more of the residents who claim to have witnessed them. True, that given the authenticity of the events, the description of the murder is supported by circumstantial evidence. But in my two years of work, of studying the beliefs, the lore, the habits, the ways of thinking of the people of Bloomville, I have been led to one inevitable conclusion: they are a people incapable of objective observation because of deep-rooted superstitions, religious beliefs, and social values.

Which is not to say that there are no grains of truth to the story. I did in fact snatch Laura from the faithful fold. We married shortly thereafter. Within the year she accompanied me back to Yale, which was I am sure an eye-opening experience for her. When I began work on my dissertation, we returned to Bloomville—her home was ours through inheritance, her mother having died six months after the wedding, her father two years later. The country home was ideal for us and for my research. Set in the rich, green hill country, it offered rest, relaxation and peace. I had a good supply of tales from the locals, and on this I based my work. Thus I found it necessary to mix intimately with the indigenous characters, visit their taverns, their homes, their churches, and indeed show a sincere interest in them, which having done successfully I now possess a fine supply of tales, one among them most remarkable.

Laura was the very woman they spoke of—frail, yes—but the beauty of her features is something I could not capture with words. Although she was a devout person, she still had preserved her innate capacity to do good acts for others, the quality of their person not always the highest. As a wife she was ideal, and I doubt that anyone loved another person more than she did myself.

A clear memory drifts up from the murk of unconsciousness. It was an idle spring day and we sat under the blossoming trees in the garden behind the house. Laura got up and picked a flower, and as she returned to me I startled her by jumping up, grabbing her about the waist, thrusting her head high into the cherry tree, white and fleecy as a low flying cloud. I let her down, caressing her breasts. She looked very beautiful to me and I told her so. I borrowed a line from *Tristan and Isolt* that aptly suited my purpose. She looked puzzled. I said, "You have within your lovely breast the key to my heart." If she heard anything in high school it was that.

"You have mine," she answered.

We lay down in the cool, soothing grass and watched the cherry blossoms fall with each burst of the spring breeze. After a few minutes, she began to laugh, and I knew I was expected to ask why. When I pressed, she responded, gazing at the tree, talking in her usual abstractions.

"Do you want to hear my philosophy of love? It won't take long."

"Very well."

"Love isn't as simple as loving someone. I've always loved you, but now it's as important that I love the love you have for me. Kind of like a double bond. Do you know what I mean?"

"It's a common enough theme."

"Oh."

"But don't let that silence you. Think of it as good poetry: 'What oft was thought but ne'er so well expressed.'"

"Pope," she said proudly.

"Right. Now to do a good job on this, aim for expression. The theme is overdone."

"You read too much," she said.

"Not all from reading," I answered, hinting at my rakish days as an undergraduate, which I discussed openly with her before.

"I'm lost, I'm afraid. You've heard it and you've heard it better."

"Whatever comes from your lips will be superior, I promise you."

She grew confident again and began. "When we were first married, I was pretty proud of being married to you— I still am of course. But then I thought that since I married someone, well, a little better than anyone else I know did, I was more deserving. You found somebody worthy of loving, and it was because of me that you were able to love. Now I see that that's wrong. You love me as you do because you have the ability to love, and that's the essence of love. The ability, not the object. You won't like this, but really, Christ is the best example of ultimate love because he could love Man even though Man was not deserving of so much love."

"That's to Man's credit," I interrupted, growing impatient with the awkward mythical analogy, despite which the scene is engraved on my mind.

"Now tell me truly," I asked half seriously. "Didn't you really marry me because of what Paul said, that the 'unbelieving husband is consecrated through his wife'?"

"No, I was just trying to be respectable about it all, I guess."

That was a milestone in our relationship, for she had brought up one bit of Paul after another between us, but now she was growing up, shedding those shreds of immaturity.

It was late April when Laura talked me into visiting old Mrs. Miller. When we walked through the dusty halls reeking of antiquity and burst upon that sad sight of a woman helpless in bed, clearly in a general state of distress, I knew that Laura would grow a good deal from the experience. For Mrs. Miller and Laura sprang from the same dry soil; on Sundays they called upon the same silent Lord. And now she would see how the Lord watched over his flock. In short, she would have to dispose of her native murk and open her eyes.

When Mrs. Miller began in her martyred but steadfast voice, "In rough times there's naught a body can do but love his God, his country, his family and friends, and bear the burden that falls on him," I nearly choked on my tea. Ah Christ, I thought to myself, the woman will yet ask why her God "haith" forsaken her. She'll shortly follow in the footsteps of the son, who would now be no more than a historical farce if Matthew's text had been properly preserved, ending as it should have with "Eli, Eli, la' ma sabach-tha'ni?" The rest of her visits were alone.

And it was not long thereafter that I began to sense the general rumblings about town. The first man to openly object to my lack of protection toward Laura was her minister, the Methodist Reverend Moore. I was in town on some business, walking down the hot, black street when I saw his great form coming toward me. He walked boldly up to me and addressed me in his usual manner, sounding as if the whole thing had just been rehearsed in the parsonage study. He was a dark, heavy man, fairly large though not yet corpulent, stern when he thought he should be, soft-spoken all other times. Now, confronted with such a heathen, he required sternness.

"Mr. Hamilton," he began, dropping his huge jaw. "I keep my nose out of your business, you keep yours out of mine. That's how we get along."

"Well said, Reverend."

"But now there's something I've got to say to you. Our paths cross out of necessity."

He offered me a seat on a bench, and I replied that it was a public bench and so he was doing me no favor.

"It's obvious to us that you're no equalitarian." He pronounced the second syllable as in "quail."

"No," I replied quickly. "I never liked birds." He took the double insult to heart as he should have.

"That may be," he responded ruffling his shoulders. "And some folks would have you run out of town for it. I'm of a different opinion, long as you steer clear of me."

"The day I set foot in your church, you may put a pistol to my head. And if when I'm as old as some of the dead wood in this town I call on the Lord as a drowning man grabs onto an imaginary straw, then send me your biggest brute—probably the one who takes up the collections—and have him beat some sense into me."

"I'd like to get to the problem at hand. Laura, you know, was always the favorite of the town. We all knew her well. We all loved her. We don't know what you do to her out there, but we do know that she's changed."

"That's good, since when we met she was a child."

"Then try to conceive what she's lost. Now the poor girl is mistreated, abused, neglected. She walks into town alone every other night. It's a mile or more and that's a hard distance for a frail girl like Laura."

"She's neither frail nor is she a girl. Once you yokels grasp that fact, you'll see things better."

"The thought of the poor girl," he began ignoring my point, "walking through that dangerous country, those old foundations, uncovered wells, streams, ravines, where bears have been seen and wild dogs abound. It chills me. God it's frightening. And you have a Mercedes Benz don't you?" he said looking up as if he just played his trump card that would bring me to my knees in defeat. "She can drive."

"Never could handle the old four-speed. She grew up you know on the column."

"Then in God's name drive her in before she's gone."

"Gone? Come now, Reverend." He had a tendency to get over-excited, which explains why he was known to have produced some rousing sermons. "There's nothing better than the walk between our house and town. The beauty of the trees, the stream, the fields…." But I realized he was drawing me further into the conversation than I

10

intended to go. It was time I got out. I'd been diplomatic long enough and did not want to begin insulting the old fool.

"Mr. Moore," I began as the heat of the afternoon gradually reached into the shade. "With the townspeople providing such close surveillance, I see no reason at all why she should be in any danger." And with that I left him.

A couple of nights later, I drove into town—Laura having walked in earlier without my knowing it. While I was there I visited Blanche's Tavern, the local haunt where I used to gather stories when I was doing research. Now, however, I wanted only a quick drink. Things had changed a good deal since I had been a regular patron. Now some of my story tellers did not greet me as they used to. One of my finest sources, Hap Malone—a very devil of a man—eyed me occasionally. I drank two scotch and waters and turned to go. But Hap came up to me and explained in his gruff and sly way that he had the finest story "I ever heared."

No I wasn't interested, I explained. He insisted, and he was among friends. I was not. So he sat me in a corner table, my back to the window that looked out to where my car was parked. He began a slow, lengthy story, part of which I had already heard, about a woman, Mrs. Druese, who killed her husband and attempted to feed him to the pigs. His head was severed and not disposed of as the rest of the body was. (These facts, by the way, are recorded in the court records.) She was the first woman hanged in the county. What finally became of his head is still unknown. Hap digressed to a story about a well-known sinkhole that periodically fills with water, where lots of things unaccountably lost are said to have disappeared. (In this respect, the sinkhole serves a function much like religion—a catchall for the unaccountable.) Well, Hap heard that the head was thrown into the legendary hole. This story—while undoubtedly false—is indeed a revelation, for it nicely illustrates how local lore, unrelated though its tales may be, tends to unite.

Hap was a talented story teller with a kind of vernacular wit, and he managed to stretch the story to a full half hour. When he was done I thanked him and got up to leave but he offered me more stories. When I refused, he grew belligerent. I tore his ugly hand from my wrist and walked quickly out the door. I had not gone more than a few steps when I saw Laura leaving the rear entrance of a large white house that did not belong to Mrs. Miller. In a second I was struck senseless, and I hid behind a building so that she would not see me, and so that no one in Blanche's would either. I felt that big glass window at my back like a giant eye.

As I sped home along the dark, wooded road, I considered more rationally the question at hand. I have always believed in the paradoxical and inexplicable nature of Man. Hence, a woman like Laura could certainly be involved in such clandestine activities even though her basic character was oriented otherwise. But before accepting the paradox, I had first to ascertain that there was one. Even an intelligent person can misread the facts. I resolved to watch in secrecy, but my plan was nearly foiled when Laura came to bed and asked me where I had driven the car. It was normally kept in the garage, and in my haste I had left it out. "A tune up," I replied with little confidence since I knew nothing about mechanics.

When she left for town a few nights later, I took the lantern and followed a good distance behind, but I lost her near town and was not about to wander the streets or stake out a house so close to Blanche's. It was a Saturday night and the hormones of the young high school students were being roused to action on this lusty evening. I was sitting in a vacant lot watching when several cars pulled up. It looked like the high school dance overflow. A girl half-dressed got out of a car and ran toward me, her boyfriend or attacker (or both) close behind. When she was nearly upon me, her lusty pursuer caught her and together they returned to the car to complete their nefarious business. A fine incident to lay before their righteous parents. I can see them now, sitting in the pew with their offspring, angelic smiles on all faces. I left and I hope escaped being seen.

That was the first time I used the lantern. The second was on a dark night the following Tuesday. But again I lost her, and when it grew late, I knew I had to be home or be exposed. She arrived shortly after, tired, her hair disheveled, her clothes in disarray. There was a kind of wanton beauty about her, and nothing would have pleased me more than to take her that very instant. Anger, jealousy and love combine to form a curious sort of passion.

At one time, two doors lay open to me. One, to find out for myself the nature of the situation. Two, to correct the problem while remaining unenlightened. One door was closed or at best ajar. My attempts at spying had failed, and since I always considered myself a better negotiator than spy, I resolved to manipulate the affair. I avoided the real issue, kept truth entirely out of it, and simply said that I had received a lot of trouble from the locals because I permitted such freedom.

"You forget," Laura answered, "that I grew up here, I know the country like I know our house. And don't pay a whole lot of attention to the locals."

She was right of course. Then I suggested spending more time at Yale, doing some post-doctoral work.

"But this is our home now. We can't just leave it, especially in the spring. The lilacs are blossoming in the yard, the flowers are in full color. Cherry blossoms haven't begun to fall. And it's so fine here in the summer, you've said that yourself. Do you want to leave?"

"No," I had to admit, for nothing was more beautiful than our country house in the spring and summer. But then there was that ugliness too, like a shadow of a dismal cloud.

Having failed at negotiating, only through my own honesty—I could have insisted that we leave—I followed her once more into town. Much before I expected it I saw her leave the rear entrance of the big white house across the street from Blanche's.

There was no doubt now, but still the opposing facts were hard to reconcile. And now, to complicate things, there were her apparent sincere feelings about our home. So there they stood, two intransigent poles pulling fiercely at each other, neither overpowering the other and neither able to stand alone in the end.

The next day was certainly one of the most enlightened days of my career as a folklorist. I had the privilege of witnessing what must be a folklorist's dream. I saw a story born, I saw it grow from its very germ. And I was part of it.

I was walking by Elwin Tillman's old shack when his brute of a mad hound bounded toward me obviously bent on destruction. Fortunately Elwin was at the door and he called the beast back. I waved to him in appreciation but he yelled back, "Hang on there young feller. I've got to have a word with ya."

"Very well, Elwin," I said. I usually did my best to be pleasant with him, for despite the fact that he was a retarded or senile (or both) old man, he was not a bad fellow.

He sucked viciously at his pipe for a second, pulled it out of his mouth (which for some reason he could not hold still) and then began.

"Seein's how yer a story collector, I got some things that might be of interest to ya. Either sit yerself down or stand up, it's all the same to me, but I'm gonna sit." I sat next to him on a felled log. "Ah 'tis a fine day, ain't it though?"

"Sure, 'tis Elwin," I agreed, for 'twas.

"Ya know the story of old Dar Sickler well enough I don't doubt."

"That I do, Elwin."

"Well, Dar were one o' them people—he weren't all bad, he weren't all good. Jist that he had a mean streak in 'im, an' if they hung 'im fer' his mean streak, they should uh praised 'im fer his good streak. He was a good man an' he never let a body down."

"I tend to agree, Elwin. It was more like he just went berserk," I said trying to keep the conversation going.

"Not at all, not at all, son. You ain't listenin' to me, but ya better listen close 'cause what I got to say is important. He wasn't crazy. He was mean at times, but he was hisself when he done in his family. That I know. But there's a mean killing streak in all of us maybe, and he's jist one which is like all of us an' we're all the same."

Elwin would occasionally soar to great heights of complexity. Sometimes the import of that statement escapes me.

"Now here's the point I think you'd be wantin' to hear," he continued. "Old Dar was a man of strong will, and when he wanted somethin' he got it." He looked at me through dull, narrow eyes as he feigned a kind of wisdom for when he had a good story he had a captivated audience and he knew it. "Well he don't take kindly to the hangin', I'll tell ya." He stood up impatiently. "Dar wasn't buried far from here." He pointed off into the green valley that ran toward home. "Now some nights he wanders through the valley. His ghost's walkin' about, by Jesus, and he's lookin' fer his head. I seen 'im a few times already head chopped clean off at the shoulders."

The valley he pointed to was the very same through which Laura walked to get to town and the same one I used when I followed. Something inside me started when I saw the connection, when I saw how murderers, headless men and jealous husbands all twine and tangle together in the minds of simple folk. This is how a story forms, and it is nothing less to them than reality.

It was a privilege walking among the dim, dusty lives of these people while not wearing the same "spectacles," seeing what they did not see, seeing through what they saw. But what fascinated me most was that here was a story, conceived in ignorance, nurtured on stupidity, and I was allowed to see it grow.

He stood up with a wild look in his cold, gray eyes and stared hard at me until, I have to admit, I was a bit frightened.

"The ghost of Dar is walkin' about," he said in a raspy whisper. "It's a cruel, vengeful ghost and it ain't gonna rest til it gets somebody. Watch out fer it," he continued more frightening in his mad way, his eyes more piercing. "Watch out Mr. Hamilton. You ain't a bad man." And with that he turned and hobbled quickly into the house.

I could not help chuckling to myself as I left, knowing that the headless man and I were the same, and so I had nothing to fear. But Elwin was always a good story teller, and he handled this one superbly. It is not without a slight chill that I recall the cold strangeness in his eyes.

When I got home, I jotted down the story in my notebook. Laura acted aloof, and despite my efforts to get at the nature of her discontent, she remained closed. I watched through leaded panes as she moped about the garden. I spied through the door window as she sat holding a wilted lilac. There was beauty in her brooding, in her solitude, and I knew that something complex was happening in her mind. That complexity, that seriousness, that seeming awareness of the unpleasantness of things irreconcilable attracted me.

I saw her coming slowly up the walk, her hair swaying slowly as in a dream as she looked down at the ground. I startled her as she entered.

"You're still firm in your secrecy?"

"No," she answered softly.

"What is it then?"

"Old Mrs. Miller." I knew that was a lie. "She's going to die soon, I'm sure of it."

"Oh?" I answered skeptically. "How long has the old girl?"

"A week."

"That's all?"

"That's why I'm going to see her tonight." She paused. "I won't be seeing her again, I guess."

"Well if she has a week, why then are you seeing her only once, and so long before the grand departing."

"I have better things to do than watch old women die."

"What have you better to do?"

"I have to live. I have to be happy. I have to have some kind of life. Time slips away so fast." She said the words with a bitterness I had not noticed in her before.

"One more time?"

"One."

She seemed uneasy as she turned slowly, awkwardly, leaving the room, several hours later, the house. She paused outside after a few steps and returned for the lantern.

I lit a cigarette, mixed a drink, turned the lights down. Dusk had fallen and a gray twilight lay about the trees. It was peaceful—the birds' songs beginning to die, the night air crying mournfully in the trees, the plaintive wail of a train whistle way off in Bloomville. And they all sparked within my mind the thought of faraway places, of uncommon romantic love, of mystery and beauty somewhere, somewhere, but so damned far off that all a man could do was drink his drink and dream. Peace, everything said. Peace, the sounds of the night cried out in unison. Peace said all the world.

Peace, but the loneliness and unrest of peace. For there was a ghost crawling in my stomach, that same ghost perhaps that made old Darwin get up and walk, a ghost that couldn't let things be.

The night cleared and brightened, and through the window I could see clearly. The moon spilled a bleak, silver light about, cold as steel, and I had to rise and go outdoors. The beauty of the night was stunning. Huge trees like ghosts gilded in the moonlight swayed gently. Unadorned beauty, natural beauty is most beautiful but it is transient. Not paintings, pictures, or poems, but only to an extent memory can capture it. It is perfect, undistorted, and of course dying, always dying.

I left the house and walked toward town, unconscious of past or future, knowing only the immediate present. I heard footsteps far off, and I hid thinking it would be Laura on her way home early. I watched from behind an old stone fence as her figure appeared, darkly dressed, walking slowly across the opposite end of a clearing. She carried the lantern but its flame was out. She seemed at peace as near as I could tell, her pace unhurried, her head upright as if she were breathing in the beauty of the night. As she neared, the moonlight on her delicate face showed the faintest hint of a smile. Her eyes seemed as big and round as the moon itself, only dark and deep, mysterious. She looked like some fairy queen of the woods, and indeed I think she was.

I changed my position and she must have heard me, for she stopped and looked over the short grass toward me. Then she turned and walked rapidly away, never glancing over her shoulder. When she reached the edge of the woods, I followed her. She dropped the lantern and began to run as I followed faster, still not sure what drove me after her. When the woods broke into field again, I had nearly caught her. She was panting heavily, running awkwardly, stumbling and losing balance. She lay perfectly still in front of me. She may have been conscious but her head was buried in the grass. Her thin, frail body trembled and heaved. Seeing her helpless I recognized a feeling of possessiveness in myself. Seeing her smooth white legs, her dress in disarray, her tender thighs wet from dew, I covered my face with my jacket, leaving a small hole for vision, and I undressed her. She gave no resistance except that she refused to cooperate, and shortly she was naked under the moonlight, shivering in the cold air. As I bent down toward her, she looked up with a vague terror in her half-closed eyes but did not scream and exhibited only minimal struggling and whimpering. I loved her then with more passion and violence than I ever had loved her before.

When I got up she lay perfectly still. I was going to leave before she became conscious and discovered her ravisher, but I noticed blood on my hands. Under the middle of her back was a sharp rook which must have damaged her spinal column. I shook her but her head rolled from one side to the other like a rag doll's. Her eyes and mouth were open, and I guessed she was dead.

I was not shocked although I was sad. I think now that death was what I had in mind for her all along. The desire, the passion were just stepping stones.

Laura and I had always been close, and I found it possible to feel that a breach was in no way created. Indeed, our last act together brought us as close as we had ever been.

Despite the coroner's report of rape and the small investigation that followed, the story, which like a mushroom growing in the primeval cave of the Bloomville mentality, sprouted and took form in a matter of weeks was that the ghost of Darwin had killed her. And while many people in Bloomville were, I'm sure, unhappy with such explanations, they never troubled me for more information.

I attended the funeral in the Methodist Church where I felt very uncomfortable. The dull eyes of Bloomville were on me. But the music was soothing, the windows, colorful and appealing. I almost wished it had been a

Catholic church—they go in for music and colors much more than Methodists do. And when the service was over I felt strongly like making the sign of the cross on myself, and I did it too, just for tradition's sake. It was all very comforting.

I dug a hole in the back yard, mostly by myself but with some help from Elwin Tillman, the only one who would venture near that evil abode. When we returned the earth to its proper place, Elwin stood silent and I expected him to shortly being grumbling in his incoherent way about how it was all my fault for not keeping her home as I should have. But he didn't. He looked at the fresh dirt and muttered, "Laura Hamilton. A good woman."

Laura's habit since that incident has been not to exhibit the reticence I expected, although I must qualify that statement in order not to imply something supernatural. It is simply that she lingers in my mind as nothing else has, as no one else could. Her presence is somehow substantiated by that white stone, visible through the dining room window. And it is not without a bit of sadness that I look on it, its firm existence somehow out of step, a precious relic of the past not properly assimilated into the thin veneer of present reality and not sufficiently remote to remove memory.

Yes, she lives in that stone was well as in my mind. But someday I'll add more life to her. I'll weave a subtle story about her life better than anything the locals have made up, and their practice exceeds mine. It won't be true of course but it will be touching, and there will be a grain of truth to it. There is something real in that.

Originally published in Four Quarters, 23.4 (Summer 1974) by the Department of English at La Salle University, Philadelphia, PA 19141-1199

THE SLABWOOD MAN

Mike Sullivan put on his red, flannel jacket and grabbed a pair of gloves from the cabinet by the door. He stretched them over his pudgy fingers. When he looked back into the cabinet where the gloves had been, he could see a bottle of Jack Daniels. He piled some wool socks around it mostly out of habit, as there was no chance Christine could see the bottle. After she lost her legs it was a lot easier for Mike to hide his bottles. It was a lot easier to hide a lot of things, but at this stage in his life, there wasn't much else to hide.

He clapped his hands in a muffled applause, hoping Christine did not hear his activities because then she'd know he was going out and would ask him to do something. He listened for her voice but heard a distant chorus outside. He almost made out a few words, but they quickly evaporated in a mist of foreign syllables. He figured the school was having a field trip and that kids were chattering as they walked along the road toward the fish hatchery.

"Mike," Christine barked from the bathroom. He slipped outside and quietly closed the door. He'd gotten out in time to say he hadn't heard her. She could always call one of the Methodist women—Agnes Bellinger or Gertrude Johansen—to help her.

A cold wind pierced his coat. He wished he had gotten his sheepskin coat out of the attic. The sheepskin coat had saved his life on one occasion when a cold snap and a binge coincided, as they often did.

The voices he heard were louder now, but the road was empty except for crisp, brown leaves whipped into the air like crippled birds by cyclones torn from the north wind. He looked up and saw that the sounds were not voices but the honking of Canadian geese chasing gray clouds that flowed like wet cement in the winter sky. More than a week ago, there was a frost. Almost every morning, he saw the vapor of his breath. In retrospect, he recognized these landmarks in the terrain of time. Winter had taken him by surprise.

It was late for firing up the sawmill. He worried that the old engine wouldn't start. The sawmill was open and cold drifted in. Freezing for Percy Hamilton and the meager salary didn't make him enthusiastic about the work, especially after Hamilton made him sign a contract to turn over his home after his death in exchange for paying Christine's medical bills. But then, they didn't have any children to leave anything to.

He plunged into the sawmill, where Hamilton's employees were doing a dance of agitation against the cold. Nobody dared touch the equipment if Mike wasn't there. Mike was an independent contractor—a carpenter, mason and sawmill operator. He contracted with the Hamiltons' little corporation that maintained the family's houses and public areas of Bloomville.

The men drank hot coffee cupped in gloved hands and inhaled the steam. They kicked the sawdust to keep up the circulation in their feet. Some spit as foreplay to the work of revving up the machinery and slicing the logs.

Richard Sealy did not spit now and never had as far as anyone knew. He was trying to fix the elastic strap of his safety glasses. Safety first, was his motto. "What good are safety glasses without good straps to hold them on," he said as Mike joined the men.

"You and your goddamned safety glasses," said Mike.

Sealy and his wife moved to Bloomville in Upstate New York this fall when she got a teaching job. Sealy had a college degree but he didn't boast about it. Even so, he stood out in Hamilton's work crew with his safety-first attitude, his know-it-all manner, and his Jehovah Witness religion. He had a way of letting everyone know that he was the only one of the work crew going to heaven. Halvar Johansen, the Norwegian supervisor, scoffed at religion but thought it was good for his wife, Gertrude. He was dying of cancer, and there was no obvious successor to his job. Everyone assumed Sealy was positioning himself to take over.

Johnny Styles was a small, wiry man who Mike considered a mindless farm hand. Farm workers didn't know much about anything off the farm and had a hard time doing what they were told. Johnny rested on his peavey the way a farmer leans on a pitchfork—with one arm crossed in front of him, his forearm on the shaft. Johnny talked a lot but had little to say. Cuss words and barnyard expressions made up his utterances. He took the Lord's name in vain in every other sentence or sentence fragment.

On Sealy's first day at work, he called Johnny a sinner. He didn't think much of Mike, a Catholic who was not going to heaven because of his drinking and because it was too easy for Catholics to be forgiven for their sins.

Elwin Denson was the work crew's only other shot at eternal bliss. He was over 70. He used the smallest lawn mower, worked the slowest, got paid the least. Elwin was the slabwood man. When the slabs of bark were sliced from the logs in long strips, he cut them into two-foot lengths and stacked the pieces in piles for the Hamiltons to use in their fireplaces and wood stoves. Sometimes he worked so slowly that the slab wood piled up and Mike had to shut down the saw to let him catch up. Although he professed no religion, Elwin seemed incapable of doing anything religion would not condone, and he could have made it in any church that didn't require a large offering.

This Saturday Halvar brought in Jimmy Bellinger, son of the English teacher, to help Elwin. During the previous summer, Jimmy worked for Mike Sullivan to save money for college. Jimmy was Mike's favorite person among the crew, and Jimmy adored Mike.

Mike disliked Sealy because he knew Sealy wanted to run the machines. Sealy was itching to get his hands on the rusty, steel lever that controlled the carriage that fed the logs into the giant saw blade. The man who controlled that lever and the smaller one that engaged the saw blade controlled the sawmill. Mike worked those levers. He sensed that Sealy was tempted to push the red starter button that hung from a beam. If he did that and got away with it, next thing you know he'd be at levers.

Mike positioned himself between Sealy and the button so he could push it and run for the levers before Sealy did. Not being much of runner, he needed a distraction.

"Richard, would you check the fuel level for me," Mike said.

"Sure. What do you put in this thing?"

"Rye and ginger," said Mike. Sealy was about to peer into the fill hole when he reared up to sling an insult at Mike. He was checked by a chorus of laughter.

"What the hell does he think we put in there," Mike said to everyone but Sealy.

"Some of these old military engines use diesel," Sealy said.

"Not the ones with spark plugs," Mike said as he punched the red button, sending the motor into spasms and coughs with bursts of blue smoke. When the engine settled to a rumble, Mike was at the lever.

Sealy put the cap back on the gas tank. "You didn't tell me you were going to start it. That's dangerous starting that thing with the tank open and my hands on the engine."

Mike laughed and motioned for the crew to come to his workstation. "Are these logs all inspected?"

Richard Sealy and Elwin Denson were responsible for inspecting the logs for old fence staples and nails. Any metal would have been covered by 100 years or more of bark and growth, but you could see a scar where the wire went in. Only Sealy was really responsible for inspections because Elwin could not see well enough.

"We pulled these trees from the woods," Sealy said. "What would make you think they had nails in them?"

"These woods were cow pastures a hundred years ago and there were trees running along the edges. Farmers used trees for fence posts. You need to inspect every log."

"They're clean," said Sealy.

When Mike turned toward the lever, the crew took their positions. Johnny turned the log on the carriage. Halvar and Richard waited in back of the blade to stack the boards or pass the slab wood to Elwin and Jimmy.

Mike pulled the handle and eased the log up to the saw blade. He held it a second, debating whether to give it another pull, but no, it was just right. Mike tested the engine. The building quivered as pulleys turned and belts flapped. The tension wheel bounced on the flying leather belt, then settled. The blade wobbled, then straightened as the engine gained speed. Everything was moving to a gentle hum. Mike put on his safety glasses, looked around at the crew, engaged the blade and pulled the lever to move the log. The blade screamed and threw sawdust into the air like wind-blown snow. The sweet smell of green life ripped from the logs filled the air and inspired the crew to work through the morning, cutting log after log into beams and boards for the Hamiltons' projects.

Now and then a cherry log went through the saw, and Mike put the blade in neutral while he, Halvar, and Johnny carried some boards behind the mill by the creek. Jimmy offered to help because he knew these were Mike's private boards. But Mike told him to take a break. When they returned, Sealy asked, "What do you do, take a commission on the wood?"

"You could call it that," said Mike.

"You don't call it anything," Halvar warned.

"I call it dishonest," said Sealy. "I call it a sin. You're stealing."

That afternoon, they were slicing a maple log. Sawdust flew as usual when the blade screamed and shot sparks that glided like fireworks to the sawdust floor. The edge of the blade turned red. Mike stopped the saw, walked over to the engine and shut it down.

"God damn it, Sealy. So you inspected the logs. Well you did a hell of a job. That nail's going to put us behind half a day if the mill doesn't burn down. Now get a bucket of water to put those sparks out."

Mike and Halvar took off the blade and four of them carried it to the shop. They built a fire in a wood stove and sat around while Mike filed the blade tooth by tooth. The rest of the crew couldn't have been doing less when Percy Hamilton pushed open the door. He wore a long, dark coat that brushed his polished shoes. "What's the matter boys? Getting too cold for you? Or is this a coffee break?"

Halvar explained. "One of the logs had a nail in it. Ve have to file the blade."

"Ve?" said Hamilton, mocking his use of the plural more than the Norwegian accent. "I see one person filing."

Sealy spoke up. "I suggest we have two blades. If one needs sharpening, we can send it out while we use the other. A commercial place could sharpen this blade quickly and we'd have less downtime."

Mike stopped filing and looked over the rim of his glasses at Sealy. "Damn you Sealy. If you'd inspected these logs, we wouldn't need two blades. We wouldn't need to sharpen this blade. You let the nail get through. That's why you're sitting on your ass."

Hamilton glared at Sealy, then turned to Mike. "How long will it take to get the blade ready?"

"A couple more hours," said Mike.

"Well boys, let's go split wood. We're expecting a cold winter and we'll need plenty of wood to burn."

As the men stood up, Johnny was the only one to speak. "Kerplunk, kerplunk," he said.

By afternoon, the blade was sharpened and the men were back to work. It was common for people to stop by the sawmill. Jimmy Bellinger's father, Roger, brought the lunch Jimmy had left home.

"Hard-working men," he said, using a sarcastic phrase sure to irritate Halvar, who disliked teachers and other people with a college education.

"Ve are men," Halvar said, poking his chest with his finger. "This is men's verk."

"You just make sure that boy doesn't get near that blade," Roger said.

"Dad, I got the lunch. You can go."

"You leave the boy to us," Halvar said. "He'll learn more here than in college."

"You'll have his mother to answer to if anything happens to him."

"Ve are not afraid of vomen here."

Mike shut down the engine and stood between Halvar and Roger. "Don't worry about the boy," he said to Roger. "I'll make sure he's safe."

Roger trusted Mike and left without another word.

Some visitors were not welcomed. No one saw Tim Tenyke stumble through the arches. Heir to a fortune in his youth, Tim squandered his money on women and drink. At least, that's the story Jimmy's mother told. She warned that if Jimmy wasn't careful he'd end up like Tim Tenyke. That was a sobering thought. Now destitute, Tim lived in a one-room cabin with only a wood stove for heat. He drank like a fish and smelled worse than one. His talk was as foul as his odor.

Mike shut down the engine again.

"Tim, we can't have you in here when we're working," Mike said.

"Just stopped by to say hello."

"Well you said it. Now you've got to move on so we can finish work."

"Well, I saw you had a kid here so I figured you wouldn't kick me out."

"The kid works here."

"Hell I'll work too. Always need some spare change."

Mike coaxed Tim away with an invitation to his house in a week or so. It was time for a break, and Mike had a question he'd been meaning to ask Johnny. "What does 'kerplunk kerplunk' mean?"

The crew broke into laugher. Seems everyone knew about this phrase except Mike and Jimmy. Even Sealy joined in with laughter. Johnny stepped forward.

"Well, see we was working at Hamilton's house, me and Halvar and Sealy, trying to unplug his septic line. So we got the cover off the distribution box and along comes Hamilton and that wife of his, Catherine, to watch. We's all standing there looking into this soup and that old pipe from the house is leaking a little stream. All of a sudden, out comes a pink rubber and drops right into the soup. Kerplunk. And another one right behind it. Kerplunk, kerplunk. Well they float around in the soup like they's tryin' to find a way out. Well, I's the only one to speak up. 'Well Jee-sus Christ,' I says. Just like that. 'Jee-sus Christ.' Well, Catherine, she turns and walks back to house, and Hamilton he sticks around looking at those pink rubbers. Finally he says, 'Well let's get this fixed, boys.' Well, gettin' it fixed ain't so easy. We's all standing there with our shovels, reluctant to dip them into that soup on aconna those two pink rubbers. I mean, shit's one thing."

Working for Hamilton was humiliating, and Johnny had devised a way of protecting what little dignity nature had provided him. For Johnny, secrets that slithered out of the sewer reduced Percy Hamilton to the level of a common man, a Johnny. "Kerplunk, kerplunk" erased the vast difference in wealth, education and brains between the two men. Just for a moment, in Johnny's mind, they were equals. Johnny never considered that Hamilton probably interpreted "kerplunk kerplunk" as the babble of the village idiot, but if he had, so much the better. It showed his ignorance.

Mike protected his dignity by swiping cherry boards, leftover bricks, a bag of mortar. It wasn't the value of the material he pilfered. He was putting one over on Hamilton. It was psychological compensation for all he had to sign over to the Hamiltons for the medical assistance they reluctantly gave Christine. As if the life she gave them and the marriage and children he went without were not enough. Mike started to admire Johnny.

* * *

Jimmy and Mike became friends over the past summer. Neither could discuss the friendship because of the chasm of years. Mike was not articulate and spoke in rough phrases. Jimmy was a kid, groping for words to express feelings he hardly understood. Mike showed Jimmy how to use woodworking tools, how to keep them razor sharp. Jimmy thrived on pleasing Mike.

Mike and Jimmy did some clandestine work too, and working in the shadows brought them closer together. After a day's work, they'd take the leftover lumber, bricks, blocks, nails, shingles and hide them behind the sawmill. He and Jimmy never talked about why it was OK.

In his spare time at the woodshop, Jimmy built a guitar. Sometimes he and Mike would take an early lunch to work on it. Mike was impressed by Jimmy's enthusiasm for woodworking. He also was impressed that Jimmy never talked about college or about being a chemical engineer someday. Jimmy feared the difference in education between his family and Mike's would drive a wedge between them.

A few months ago, on the last day of work before school started, Mike was on a scaffold fixing bricks in a chimney in one of the Hamiltons' houses. He passed the mortarboard to Jimmy and asked for more mortar.

"How much?" Jimmy asked.

"Oh a sizable gob," Mike said.

Jimmy felt he should know what a sizable gob was, but he didn't. He carefully measured a lump of mortar, put it on the board, studied it and passed it up to Mike. "Was that right?" Jimmy called.

"Just right, Jim," said Mike.

That afternoon, they quit work early and went to the woodshop. Mike told Jimmy to sit on an old chair near the band saw, and he returned with a bottle of whiskey.

"Would you like a nip of the old bottle," Mike asked.

"Sure."

"Now you don't want to mention this to your mother or father. Especially your mother."

"My father gives me beer. And he drinks more than he lets on. In the winter, I see the yellow holes in the snow."

"Your father's a smart man. Won't touch the hard stuff. But he's always got a cold bottle around and a church key to open it. Well this isn't beer. This is the real thing."

Mike opened the bottle and drank, then passed it to Jimmy. "Take a swig."

Jimmy tipped the bottle straight up. The bubbles roll up through the neck, through the brown liquid. "Easy," Mike said taking the bottle. "This isn't beer, I told you." Jimmy shivered from the burning, but quickly warmth flooded his veins. His toes felt numb and his scalp tingled. They talked for a while about the Hamiltons, about the guitar project, about the logs that were coming in from the woods. Then Mike took a small wooden object out of his pocket.

"I made this from a piece of rosewood you left here. Hard as rock. I turned it on the lathe and polished it like glass. It's the most beautiful wood I've ever seen. I put a hole through the top so you can wear it around your neck."

Jimmy held it up. "What is it? Looks like a bottle."

"Well I'll grant you that it does, but it wasn't my intent to make a bottle. Everything on a lathe comes out round. It's for you to remember me, and the bottle is not what I want you to remember. It's like a charm."

"Good luck charm, like the luck of the Irish."

"Yea, the luck of the Irish."

Then Jimmy took a sharp turn. His father had talked about how Mike and his nephew, Patrick, had to leave Ireland, and it had to do with a racehorse. But his father had provided no details.

"So why did you leave Ireland?" he said.

"Well, to join Christine. You see, Percy Hamilton's father and mother went to Dublin looking for a nanny. They offered good money, or it looked like good money when you were in Dublin. I followed her. And I tell you that no one loved the Hamiltons more than Christine did. They were her family and her children."

"I heard something about a racehorse."

"Well there was that too about the racehorse."

"Is it a secret? Because nobody seems to know about it."

"Nobody asked. Would you like another swig? Can't fly on one wing."

That night at dinner, Jimmy was talking fast and incoherently. He told his sister how Mike had asked for a sizable gob of mortar and how he had guessed the size.

"Well how big is a sizable gob?" his sister, Jackie, asked.

"About the size of an average cow turd."

"Gee Christmas," his mother, Agnes, said, setting down the serving bowl of spaghetti with a whack. "We don't need that kind of bathroom talk at the table."

Jimmy ignored her. "I know something you don't."

"Well I hope you do," his father said.

"I know why Mike Sullivan left Ireland."

"It had to do with a racehorse," his father said.

"Yea, but what about the racehorse? You don't know that."

"I don't know that anybody knows that except Mike."

"I know it."

"How do you know?"

"Mike told me. How the hell do you think I know? From the horse's mouth."

"You sure that's the end you were talking to?"

"Just a minute," Agnes interrupted. "You don't need to curse at the table."

"I didn't say horse's ass," his father said.

"Not you. It's his language and going on about what somebody did wrong that they had to leave Ireland." She turned to Jimmy. "This work with those men is not doing you any good. Well school starts Monday and you'd better get out of your system whatever you have in it, mister."

Jimmy smiled.

"Well, Mike had this friend who had a slow racehorse outside of Dublin. And he had this friend who had a real fast horse that raced in Dublin and won all the time. And Mike noticed that the two horses looked alike. So he borrowed the fast horse and ran him in a race in this place outside Dublin as if he was the slow horse. He and Patrick bet every cent they had on the horse. The horse won and they won a lot of money. By the time the people figured out what they'd done, they were on a ship for New York."

"So he's a swindler on top of being a drunk," Jimmy's mother said.

Mike was a drunk. He would stay off the bottle for months but then give in with a vengeance. He'd be seen staggering down the road with his zipper open or driving his car into the creek. Or almost dying in a cold snap. The most serious binge occurred a year ago just after the old hotel burned down. The siren went off in the volunteer fire department, and Mike and his nephew, Patrick, answered the call. The volunteers were not prepared for a big fire. They met once a month to train but usually watched dirty movies instead. Rarely was there a fire still burning by the time they got there. But the old hotel was half a block from the fire station, and it was ablaze when the volunteers arrived. They began dragging hoses to the building. Mike suggested to Patrick that they change their strategy from fire suppression to salvage. Patrick dropped the hose, and they made for the cellar entrance, tore open the doors and went into the smoky basement. The walls were piled high with cases of liquor. They made one trip after another, carrying the cases to Patrick's station wagon and sampling on the way. "To make the load lighter," Mike would say. When the station wagon was nearly full, the two were maneuvering precariously. They left the basement carrying a large case of gin, and the fire hose Patrick had dropped on the ground was among the things they didn't see. Both tumbled into the snow.

"Damn it, Patrick," Mike said as he watched the orange flames light up the night sky. He tried to get up. "I got to hold onto the ground to keep from falling off."

If that hotel had not burned, Mike might have remembered what he did for the next few days. Christine sounded the alarm a day after his last sighting. The men searched the woods around town and queried neighbors. The afternoon of the third day, Elwin Denson appeared at the main road dragging Mike. He called for help and within minutes, neighbors carried Mike into the store and laid him next to the wood stove. The story of the rescue spread, and Elwin was labeled a hero.

"I was just walking through the woods in back of the red barn when I saw him in a hollow under an elm tree," said Elwin. "I ain't no hero. I saw my duty and I done it."

Mike acknowledged that Elwin saved him, but one morning during a coffee break at the bowling alley he changed his story.

"If I hadn't had on my sheepskin coat, I'd a perished," he said. "And if I'd been sober, I'd have frozen. But then, if I'd been sober, I wouldn't have gone to sleep in the woods I guess."

Father Brendan, Patrick's brother, was called to give the pledge to Mike, who made another solemn oath never again to drink. The first sip he took after that pledge was on the day he and Jimmy shared a few swallows of Jack Daniels. Later he put the bottle in the cabinet by the door and tried not to touch it.

* * *

In the cold of the sawmill, the men were getting anxious. Halvar was sick and would not return to work. Richard Sealy had taken over. He looked toward the Sullivan house to see if Mike was coming, but the dirt road was empty. He pushed the red button that started the engine and walked over to the controls. The crew didn't take their positions. They watched Sealy fiddle with the lever that engaged the blade. Jimmy stood up and looked past the jagged blade. Sealy inched the small lever toward him, searching for the spot that would engage the clutch and spin the blade. Jimmy ran toward Sealy to try to stop him. In an instant Jimmy's hand grasped the lever while his shoulder collided with the blade.

Sealy let go of the lever and jumped back. The blade wobbled to a stop. Johnny ran to Jimmy, who was lying in front of the blade. Elwin killed the engine.

Mike was just leaving his house when he heard the engine start, then stall. The commotion of voices told him there was trouble at the sawmill. He jogged along the dirt road and through the arched entry. The crew stood around Jimmy. His clothes were bloody and Sealy was peeling off his coat.

"God damn it," said Mike pushing his way to Jimmy. "Jimmy you okay? What the hell happened?"

"Looked to me like the blade was barely turning when the kid hit it," said Johnny.

Jimmy just held his shoulder like he was trying to keep his arm in place. Sealy pulled off the bloody sleeve.

When Sealy wiped away the blood, the injury was less than anyone expected. A row of puncture wounds ran across his shoulder.

"Johnny was right," said Sealy. "The blade was hardly turning." Sealy gave him a stern look. "You're a pretty lucky kid who did a stupid thing. You almost lost an arm."

"Yea," said Jimmy rubbing his arm. "And you're a moron."

"I want to know what happened," Mike demanded.

"I'll tell you," said Johnny. "This damn fool he decides he's gonna run the mill and he doesn't know a horse's ass about it. We's all just sittin' where we was, you know like we wasn't going to have any part of it, and Jimmy here he runs to stop him. Well this moron— Sealy—lucky thing he don't know how far to move the lever so he couldn't get the blade turning when the kid runs his shoulder into it."

"Well, this could have been a lot worse," said Sealy. "But if you want to know what saved his arm, it's sloppy maintenance. The linkage to the clutch has gotten so slack that you have to move the lever quite a ways to engage it. I hadn't moved it that far when the kid came at me. I guess the Lord works his miracles in strange ways."

"Sloppy maintenance—you somonabitch," said Johnny. "You got some explaining to do to this boy's parents."

"I'll do the explaining," said Mike. "This boy's my responsibility. I'll take him home and get him to a doctor."

"I'm responsible," said Sealy.

"You're responsible for being a moron," said Jimmy.

Jimmy was feeling good about his assault on Sealy but he wasn't sure why. He was proud to defend Mike against Sealy and his ilk. As they got into Mike's Jeep, Jimmy knew his work at the sawmill was over. He imagined a day when he would come home from college for a summer. He imagined Richard Sealy would be running the operation. Halvar would be dead. Jimmy would pay Mike a visit, expecting to stay a long time. They would sit at the cherry table in the dining room and talk about the things they did that summer and fall. Jimmy would make some jabs at Hamilton and Sealy that were sure to draw approval from Mike. They would talk about the liquor they drank that day in the wood shop. But soon the conversation would go flat, and with nothing left to say, Jimmy would shake Mike's hand and say good-bye.

Back home, Jimmy's mother would say something like, "Did you pay Mike a visit? I'm glad you did. He always asks about you."

Jimmy watched the landscape fly by in a blur of gray trees and white snow. He pictured Mike and the work crew in faceless silhouettes that in time would silently fall over, one by one by one.

He wondered what he would be after college when they were gone. Maybe he'd be a poor drunk but loyal man who got his start with alcohol with an aging alcoholic. Or worse, a Tim Tenyke, who blew his money drinking liquor and chasing women, a lifestyle that did not seem all that bad at the moment.

Jimmy's life was linked to Mike's in a way he only was beginning to understand. Like Mike, he would one day meet the likes of Percy Hamilton and his surrogate, Richard Sealy. He would despise them despite the financial rewards they could throw his way. It was too late to change his attitude about such people, who he realized might have power over him one day. He felt the rosewood charm around his neck, and imagined that Mike would be with him in tough times. He felt afraid to be alone.

Mike asked why Jimmy attacked Sealy. Jimmy explained that Sealy had no right to run the sawmill without Mike's permission.

"In a way he does," Mike said. "The mill belongs to the Hamiltons now. The sawmill collapsed during that snowstorm a few years ago. Percy Hamilton comes to me and tells me he wants to keep the town the way it was with the old buildings and all. He paid me for the land and paid me to supervise the work crew to rebuild it, and I signed the title over to him. So you see, Percy Hamilton can decide who runs it, and I guess he decided that Richard Sealy would be in charge since I was a bit under the weather this past week. I won't forget what you tried to do for me. I just don't want to see you ever endanger yourself for anyone. You got a big future ahead of you, and sawmilling isn't part of it."

When Mike put on the brakes at the village's only stop sign, a bottle of Jack Daniels slid out from under the seat. When he accelerated, it slid back. He winked at Jimmy. "For medicinal purposes."

The crew cut logs throughout the week. As the cold set in, Hamilton stopped by more frequently, pushing the crew to get the wood cut so they could fix the bridge and a couple roofs before the weight of snow collapsed them. No matter how much wood they cut, it wasn't enough for Hamilton. After he chewed them out one day, Mike muttered that they were working as hard as they could. Hamilton turned to walk away. Then he looked back at Mike as if a thought had occurred to him.

"Oh yes, some of the cherry boards got stacked in the wrong pile, the one behind the mill. Maybe you could see that these get in the right pile Mike?"

Mike looked him in the eye and said, "kerplunk, kerplunk."

He was surprised that Hamilton looked right back. His face turned red. Then he cast an icy stare to Johnny. Sealy stepped behind a beam as if he hadn't heard anything.

* * *

One day after school, Jimmy stopped by the sawmill. He expected to see Mike at the controls, but Sealy was running the sawmill. Jimmy saw Elwin working in back of the saw, helping to carry and stack boards. At the end of the line, where the slab wood was cut, he saw Mike Sullivan. Jimmy watched for a moment, waiting to catch Mike's eye, but Mike avoided his look. Jimmy waved to Mike until Mike couldn't help but notice. Mike tossed a feeble wave in return.

Not long after that visit, Jimmy's mother spent a lot of time at the Sullivan house. She was helping Christine, Roger said. Jimmy knew what that meant.

Mike was in bed and a team of women led by Agnes Bellinger and Gertrude Johansen took shifts watching him. They called in Father Brendan to administer another oath, but he said Mike was too far gone to know what he was swearing to, although he did swear. Looking after Mike meant going through the places he might hide bottles, starting with the bed, then the cabinets and closets, drawers and cupboards. Then they waited for Mike to come around. He remained in a stupor. When the women surveyed the bedroom a second time, they found two empty bottles.

Tim Tenyke had stopped by a couple of times but seemed to have left nothing but his stench. He came by a third time wearing the same ragged plaid hunting jacket and worn out boots. His shifty eyes took cover behind thick eyebrows. Baling twine held up two or three layers of pants. He smelled of hard cider, urine, sweat and smoke. "Come to see Mike," he said, discharging tobacco on the floor.

Agnes went up behind him, held her breath, and plunged her hands into his coat pockets, pulling out two liquor bottles.

"Holy jumpin' Moses," she said. "You old bastard. You could be responsible for this man's death."

"Just trying to help a friend."

"You get out of this house and don't come around here again. You're a good-for-nothing drunken bum," she screeched.

She opened the door and stood back so Tim and his odor could pass.

"Oh yea, kick old Tim in the ass. Let me tell you, honey, in my day I rolled dozens of women like you." He walked out to the porch. "I could have bought you when I had money." Agnes followed him, raised her leg and planted her foot on his butt.

He tumbled down the steps and onto the snow-covered sidewalk. Then he stood up, teetered until the ground stabilized, and shuffled off.

Mike slowly came out of his stupor and by Thursday, he was almost ready to work. Everyone in town heard how Agnes banished Tim Tenyke. Tim hadn't been seen in town since that day. At first people laughed about it, but by Sunday they started asking if maybe he was so scared he left town—unlikely since he didn't have a car or a destination. The weather had been frigid, so Roger Bellinger and Mike Sullivan decided to check on him. They took Jimmy with them. They parked near his cabin, then walked through the snow. There were no tracks, and snow had drifted against the door. It was as cold inside as it was outside. No fire burned in the wood stove. Tim Tenyke lay in bed frozen, a thin plastic tube on his chest. It led through a hole in the wall.

"It stinks in here," said Jimmy.

"And he hasn't even started to decompose," his father said.

The three went outside and followed the tube to a wooden barrel standing on end. Roger pulled out the tube and watched the liquid drip. Mike turned away, afraid that even the smell of alcohol would tempt him.

"That's the hardest damned cider you're going to find anywhere," Mike said. He explained that as the temperature dropped, the cider froze but not the alcohol. It collected in the center of the barrel. With each draw on the tube, Tim Tenyke sucked himself closer to his demise.

"At least he died doing something he enjoyed," said Roger. "You don't think this was Agnes's fault?"

"Hell no," said Mike. "It was the cold."

They considered the implications of Tim Tenyke's death.

"Are we going to tell the truth about this, the drinking to death," Mike asked.

"We have to," Roger said. "We have to report this to the authorities. We can't lie."

"Maybe we could just remove the tube."

"We can't even do that."

"Too bad. The truth is going to come down on us pretty hard at home. We're never going to hear the end of this," Mike said, putting his hand on Jimmy's shoulder. "Roger, you don't really think the sheriff's going to waste time on an inquiry on Tim Tenyke do you?"

"I guess not," Roger said.

"Okay. So we take out the tube and nobody says a word. Natural causes. Agreed?"

"Sure," said Roger. He looked at his son.

"Not a word out of me," said Jimmy.

BACK HOME IN THE CATSKILLS

The promise Agnes made that day at her parents' farmhouse was a forever promise. Fred looked up at his wife with sad adoration. He seemed helpless, as he often did when they were close. He was not a strong man, and when he showed his deepest feelings, he seemed weak and utterly dependent. Agnes propped him up, as she had many times before. She liked propping him up, psychologically and physically, although she was unsure why back then.

This was her moment, and for once her family let her take charge. George, her chronically drunken father, said not one abusive word. A stain of compassion seeped through his weathered face. Agnes's mother, Margaret, whose conversations had become mindless from the many years of being considered mindless, did not utter even one mundane statement. Ethel, the younger sister and a beauty, hid her vanity and resisted tossing her wavy, red hair. Ethel's husband, Al, who could usually find shallow humor in any situation, came as close to introspection as his mind allowed.

This was Agnes's moment, her time to rise in the family to the place of supreme responsibility, a place she earned by getting a college degree, by marrying a handsome and intelligent man, and by guiding her marriage through the separation of war.

Many years later, sitting on a wicker love seat on her tiny porch on a hot and deathly still afternoon in Fort Myers, Florida, Agnes recalled the scene at the farmhouse with remarkable clarity. It seemed a lifetime ago. She picked up a small cup of tea she had sipped to make the hours rush by and thought of her mother and father, dead these many years. She didn't need to fix her mind on Fred at that moment, for he had never left her thoughts. She would muse about that moment in the farmhouse as long as time allowed, as long as the phone was silent and the call she was waiting for did not come. Her gaze rested on the steamy bay as she absently watched the seagulls cross her field of vision framed by the condo porch on the seventh floor. Her mind was at home in the Catskills of New York State. Many good people and some not so good ones had gone since then.

Sorting through recollections she finally realized why Fred's dependence had meant so much to her back then. It gave her security, the assurance that he wouldn't leave her. He couldn't leave her because he needed her. That dependence was better than a promise that he would always be with her. People break promises but needs do not go away. She realized so many things about herself now that she didn't understand at that time in the Catskills. She felt embarrassed at the private revelations. Her cheeks burned with the realization that she had been, well, selfish and possessive. Her lips curled up in a hint of a smile, pushing up her sagging cheeks, adorned with rouge in anticipation of a hospital visit. Her eyes twinkled. She kept Fred on a short leash those days when they were dating and later when they were married.

Fred played in a dance band, and she tolerated that most of the time. She played in a symphony, so it was hard to deny him his musical outlet. But on New Year's Eve, she refused to let him out, and the big band played less one trombone. A handsome musician could get into a lot of trouble on New Year's Eve without a wife to manage him, and managing him was not what she intended to do on a holiday that was traditionally a family night. "Togetherness" was her favorite word, and she wasn't about to go to a dance as chaperone and watch revelers drink themselves into oblivion. She didn't appreciate drunkenness because she never drank.

Fred didn't consider himself a great musician, but he was a good one. Better, more talented musicians were temperamental and unpredictable, arriving drunk or late for gigs, or not arriving at all. He was in demand for the big bands that played proms and socials in Upstate New York because he always arrived on time and remained sober until the dance was over. Then he'd pull out a warm Genesee beer from a brown paper bag hidden in his trombone case. By the time he was home he'd have had another, seldom more than two, at least not in the beginning.

Agnes endorsed his assessment of mediocrity as a musician and mediocrity in everything else. He had just enough talent to make him attractive but no genius to make him eccentric or uncontrollable. While thinking about him as she looked out over the bay, she wondered if his talent exceeded her assessment. She wondered if she had deliberately suppressed his talents, and if he had appeased her by not being outstanding. Fred's brother, Bill, after all, was an accomplished musician who played in the clubs of New York after the war. He was a former Navy captain with a warship and five marriages in his past. "All of them good ones," he liked to say, knowing how that would irritate Agnes's traditional sense of marriage. Fred wasn't like his brother. She nodded as she put down her teacup.

When they met at Ithaca College, she knew he was the man. They studied and played music, and talked about musicians. They loved Wagner, Strauss and others, mostly Germans, and they loved music with brass. Fred was tall and flashy, with wavy black hair that shined liked polished shoes. He was a family man by any measure. He loved his mother and wrote to her in Rochester every week. Agnes was at first jealous of this mother she'd never met, but she recognized Fred's devotion as sign of good character. Fred did not mention his father, and Agnes did not ask at first. When she did, she learned that his father had died in an accident when he was child. She guessed Fred was six or seven at the time because he told her how he saved his pennies during the Depression to buy his father a piece of candy. His father was hard-working and responsible, a tailor and a Freemason. He sang tenor in the church choir.

She hadn't known a father like that. Growing up, she had a vague fear that all men were alike, and all men were like her father. George was the son of German immigrants who built a farm in the Catskills. He worked construction in New York City while living on the farm he inherited. He was a drinker and a hell raiser, a man feared by friends and enemies for his volatile personality. He was a big man with a broad, flat forehead under thick hair that turned from ash to white while Agnes was away at college. His nose curled down like an eagle's beak, and his chin was large and square. He walked with stiff legs and swung his arms as if their motion would help propel his big frame.

Agnes used to hear the yelling in the bedroom and the next day she'd watch Margaret dutifully preparing breakfast despite a bruised arm or a swollen eye. George took out his anger on others, especially if they were different or had a weakness. From George, Agnes learned that Jews were kikes and Catholics were cross backs. Germans were krauts, and Italians were wops, among other things. Just about everybody belonged to some ethnic group that George had a name for, except George, who was of course German until after the war. Then he became Swiss, as did Agnes, except when she talked about music. Then she was as German as Richard Wagner.

While Agnes was in college, her sister, Ethel, and Al married. Al complemented the family perfectly. He commuted with George to New York to the construction sites. Al knew George as well as anyone and got along with him better than most. They drank together, hunted together, fixed cars together and played tricks on each other, although they didn't laugh much. Agnes felt alienated from the family because she left home and for few years remained single while Al bonded with her father.

Agnes lacked the courage to invite Fred home to meet the parents. George didn't have much use for people who went to college. That was evident when Agnes brought her roommate, Meredith, home at Christmas break of her first year. Agnes warned Meredith not to let on that she was Jewish or she'd hear about it from George. If he got bad, they'd just go out walking in the woods or along the dirt roads, where they could talk and be alone. At dinner the first night, the dining room was a cozy, family setting. The woodstove warmed them as the country meal was served. The dining room table was unusually fancy, and the dinner of steak and potatoes was served on china with silverware Agnes had not seen before. George was unusually polite and pleasant, and Agnes was at first proud of her father. But as his charm persisted, she knew it was out of character. Finally George gently set down his knife and fork and looked straight at Meredith. "I'd a served you pork if I'd knowed who you was." He dumped a beer down his throat. "You think you can fool me with a nose like that?"

Agnes cried that night and many more. She vowed that none of her other friends would meet her father. When she and Fred got serious, she made up one story after another about not being able to go home. Finally Fred asked if she was an orphan. Agnes started dropping hints that her father was an unsavory fellow. Finally she just spilled out her feelings, her words punctuated by tears.

"My father is a hard drinker and a bad man in many ways. He's a rough guy, I mean rough around the edges. He's mean. My father is a hunter, a fisherman, not just during the season. All the time. I don't like any of those things about him, but that's what he is, and he is my father. I don't think you two should meet. I can't really picture you shooting animals much less gutting them and skinning them and hanging their heads all over the walls.

"Let me tell you what my house is like. Every wall in every room in that old farmhouse has deer heads. There's no place you can go and not be watched by those dark glass eyes. Antlers are all over the place, in drawers, on the piano, in the closets. George has so many guns he's filled five gun racks and every corner of the bedrooms. I don't know the names of all those guns. There's 30.06, 30 30s, 12 gauge shotguns, double barrels, over-and-unders, and levers and pumps and, ghee Christmas, I don't know what all. We have boxes of shells lying around. Empty shells are all over the lawn because he stands on the lawn and shoots at whatever he thinks is moving. My mother shutters every time she looks at a weapon, but she stopped complaining a long time ago.

"The way he horses around with his drunken friends, every once in a while a gun goes off in the house. Almost every room has a bullet hole. My mother keeps a jar of assorted corks around to plug the holes. They're different sizes depending on the gun. A 12-gauge shotgun left a hole near the chair rail in the dining room that's plugged with a large cork for a thermos jug. That was 12 years ago or more. The cork's still there like he's proud of the hole. Rifle holes took smaller corks but the bullets went through more walls. Bullet holes in the roof were repaired from the outside, but the holes remain in the ceiling. Mom couldn't reach them. Dad fixes the shattered windowpanes with tape until it gets cold. Then he changes the glass. He gets together with his friends and with Al, my sister's husband, and they drink on the porch until they can't see. Then they start shooting."

Fred was amused. "Well let's go meet the old bastard. I'm ready."

"Oh no, you're not ready to meet my father."

It was fall in the Catskills and George was gearing up for legally killing deer. It wasn't as much fun that way, wearing that deer license and wiring it to the antlers of the kill, taking the carnage home in daylight fully visible in the back of the truck. But George could enjoy anything if he had enough to drink.

George handed Fred a rifle with a scope and asked him if he knew what to do with it. "I'll learn," said Fred. It was a smart thing to say because George tolerated humility and hated arrogance. He, Al and a couple of Al's ilk from town donned their red, plaid hunting coats with deer licenses attached to the backs of their jackets with giant safety pins. They put on their matching hats and waited for Fred to do the same.

"You see this red?" George said poking his chest with his thumb. Fred nodded. "This is what a deer don't look like. If you see red, don't fire that goddamned thing unless you're so bad a shot that you miss anything you aim at and hit whatever you try not to."

"I'm a lousy shot," Fred said. "I'll aim at you."

"Shoot the sumunabitch," Al shouted. "That's what I always wanted to do. We won't miss him."

George walked so close to Fred his curved nose nearly bumped Fred's baby face and his whiskey breath seeped out like vapor from a smoke stack. George held his gun horizontally between them. He wiggled his mouth like was going to spit tobacco. With his eyes fixed on Fred, he jerked back the bolt of his rifle with a snap of steel and jammed a shell into the chamber. The gun's action was only an inch from Fred's groin, and his hips snapped back involuntarily. George grinned.

"Let's get some deer."

Within a few days, they had killed their limit. Fred didn't kill a deer, but George used his tag for a second one. Fred pitched in and helped gut and cut up the deer. When they were finished with the last one, they feasted on venison washed down with liquor.

The next day Al and Fred were acting like siblings. Agnes heard them plotting on the porch, but she couldn't make out the scenario. Then George joined them. They handed him large glasses of drink. Agnes was certain the glass was filled with very hard cider. Soon George was drunk. Fred and Al were sneaking their drinks from the kitchen, where they refilled their glasses with water and maintained sobriety. When George slipped the bonds of coherence, they prodded him to tell some of his most outrageous and least accurate stories. Their laughter in response was unmistakable mockery of the drunken man. Agnes watched helplessly through the screen door to the gray porch as the pantomime worked its way to a bad ending. When George suspected the plot, he grabbed Al's glass. He took a sip and spit the water out. Al grabbed Fred's arm, and they ran toward the barn. George stumbled after them, his bellowing audible but his words unclear to Agnes. They were well ahead of George when he reached the Model A pickup truck. Agnes saw blue smoke blow out the exhaust pipe, and the truck lurked toward the pair. The truck was almost upon them when they climbed up a haystack. She could see them panting as they caught their breath at the top. George furiously drove in circles around the haystack so fast that there was no window of escape. The truck went round and round the haystack in dizzying circles for half an hour until it sputtered out of gas. Agnes could see George's head resting on the steering wheel behind the silver framed window.

Fred and Al tumbled down the haystack and cautiously approached the truck. In a moment, they bolted for the house, laughing. Inside, they seemed oblivious to Agnes's anxiety.

"What is the point of doing that?" she pleaded. "You know what he's like. Al, you of all people know what he's like."

"We're just having some fun," said Al. "He won't even remember it. He'll try to figure out why the truck's got no gas in it."

"You know when he gets like that he could kill you. You just make him worse."

Fred paid no attention to her. He held a beer and asked Al for a church key. Before giving up the opener, Al reached over and turned the can upside down. "Open the bottom," he said and winked. Fred complied and over the next few hours, Agnes saw that they opened all their beer cans upside down. When the cans were empty, they put them in the refrigerator right side up.

The next morning, all the family except George were seated at the breakfast table. When George came down the stairs, he made no mention of the events of the previous day. Al and Fred watched as he walked around the table and into the kitchen. They grinned when he opened the refrigerator door. George cursed and an empty beer can hit the wall. Then another. George had discovered that the beers he thought would complement his breakfast were empty and he was the victim of another prank.

Al and Fred pushed back their chairs and ran outside. George missed his chance to catch them because he paused to pick up a rifle. He inserted a clip and jammed a cartridge into the chamber as he followed. He was aiming close to ground level when he fired five shots. Then he took careful aim and fired another. He could have hit them but he didn't.

Later that morning the pair crept back to the house to find that a fishing trip down to the creek was planned, and

George had forgiven them. He was sober and likely to stay that way. It was Sunday, and the stores could not sell alcohol. Agnes took the 8 millimeter camera she and Fred had just purchased. They took turns filming. The fishing trip and the film they made that vibrant summer day in the Catskills was engraved in Agnes's mind. It was a special time because everyone seemed happy, harmonious, and sober. If she just could have convinced her father not to drink again, her life and the lives of others would have been different. Everything would have worked out. The peace, the happiness, the togetherness, the love she felt that summer day at the creek and captured on film would have lasted a lifetime.

The chill in the November air lingered that Sunday, and Agnes and Fred were getting ready to leave. George and Margaret walked down the stone steps to the driveway with them. George and Fred were the last to say good-bye. George squeezed Fred's hand until it hurt, and he looked into Fred's face searching for a sign of pain. "You know, I had you pegged as a real candy ass," he said still squeezing the hand. "But you're going to be OK." Fred nodded and smiled. Agnes did not. On the way home, Fred couldn't stop talking about what a character George was and how great it was to go hunting and fishing and hiking in the woods with his father-in-law to be.

He reached into a paper bag where he had an opened can of beer. He held it between his legs when he wasn't sipping it. When he was sipping, he drove with his knees on the wheel, a technique he learned from George.

"I'd have given anything to have grown up in the country," he said, easing the car around a left turn with his right knee. "Right here in the Catskills. Rochester was a beautiful place to grow up, but there's nothing like the country. I love it. We are going to live in the country. Somewhere just like this. Maybe with a farm, an animal or two. A couple chickens. Maybe Thanksgiving we'll go back."

"Maybe we will," said Agnes.

They returned to farmhouse in the Catskills many times and were married there two years later. As Fred promised, they moved to the country, to the small town of Bloomville, where both were hired to teach. It was just three hours away from Agnes's parents. They worked there until the war started, when Fred joined the Coast Guard with the opportunity to play in the Coast Guard band. He hated living in Brooklyn, but he loved wearing that white uniform, playing trombone in war rallies and coming home to Agnes every night. He wanted children then, but she wanted to wait until the war was over. He might get shipped out and not come back. What would she do with a child?

"Never," he said. "The band will never be disbanded."

But the band was disbanded. It happened one glorious day in the spring of 1942 when an admiral was reviewing the band members who stood at attention, instruments in hand, before the start of a Memorial Day parade and war-bond rally. A drummer in the second row poked the musician in front of him with a drum stick, causing him to lurch forward and bump the admiral's chest. Without a pause, the admiral continued down the line. Everyone was relieved when he left without saying a word about the incident. The next day, the band members got new orders. Fred was assigned a fireman position on a troop transport ship. He was to leave for India in a month. Throughout the war he made three trips to the East to bring back troops. Not once did he play the trombone.

* * *

Many years later Agnes had a private place in her Fort Myers condominium where she kept her letters, papers, mementos—things she rarely looked at, content to know that they were there. Lately, however, she started sifting through them. Among the memorabilia were a few contemporary items, including a thank you from the Sierra Club for helping fight a nuclear power plant, and a photo of John Kerry and John Edwards with their arms raised in a victory stance. She had secretly donated quite a bit of money to them without telling her second husband, Harry Watson. If Harry had found out about the contributions, he would have chewed her out for weeks. So she hid letters along with her past. He knew about her environmental and political activism, but as long as she kept a low profile about town, he wouldn't fight her over it.

Agnes was looking for something as she pushed aside letters, photographs and programs. There it was, a black metal reel with the words "Fishing at the creek," in Fred's handwriting.

She pointed the movie projector at the bare wall, threaded the film and turned down the lights.

A young Agnes is effervescent with happiness and even slightly provocative in those flickering scenes on old color film. She wears a plaid shirt tied in a knot in front of her navel and light shorts. Her hair is silky black with bouncing curls. She is overacting for the camera, compensating for the lack of sound, as she spins around and walks away down one of two parallel ruts in the red Catskill clay. The pole with hook and sinker wags over her right shoulder.

At the fishing hole, she sits on a grassy cushion that curls over the eroded clay bank, her legs swinging against exposed earth. She is gripping the pole with her right hand. Her line is in the water, and her left hand is holding the line. She yanks the pole up, then snaps her fingers in an exaggerated gesture when the empty hook pops out of the water.

Now the camera is on George, but he waves it away with a clumsy motion of his huge hand. On apparent prompting from Agnes, now behind the camera, he opens his wicker fishing basket to a close-up that frames more than half a dozen brook trout, their glistening bodies mixed with blades of dark grass. When the camera pulls back, George is grinning awkwardly.

Now Fred is in the picture to George's right. He opens his basket and it is empty. He shrugs his shoulders, then reaches over and tries to take a few fish from George's basket. George stops him with both hands and slaps him on the back of the head. They stand motionless posing but unwilling to put an arm around each other, which is what the camera is waiting for. Then the scene goes stale and the film runs out. The light on the wall flickers. Tiny fingers of the projector chatter in search of more film, and Agnes's mind gropes in the dark for scenes of a life that is gone. She stares at bits of magnified dust sliding over the bright rectangle on the wall like paralyzed worms crawling over white earth.

Agnes rewound the film and packed it away in her closet. She opened one of the boxes of memorabilia and set it inside. In the same box, on the top of a pile of papers was the funeral service for her father. She looked it over absently. There was not a hint in the program that George's memorial service made local history as the only funeral anyone knew of where no one seemed to regret losing a family member. Friends and family came to the farmhouse. Nobody had much good to say about George. Everybody blamed his bad conduct and death on his drinking.

"He sure was a prick," Al said to a small, sympathetic audience after the memorial service. "I loved him in a way. He was my father-in-law, but God was he a prick. Inside he was a good man, you know, but when he got drunk, he was mean as hell and there weren't many times he was sober."

Margaret was well into her fifth glass of Manischewitz. She wasn't holding up her head very well.

The glaze on her eyes wasn't from crying. Margaret was the first at the funeral to mention Fred.

"I know one person who would have missed George—Fred," she said. "He really loved George. I wish Fred was here now to say something good about George. The rest of us, we're just too damned honest and too damned tired of him. But if Fred was here, he could say something good and mean it."

Al seized the moment to prop up George's legacy. "Right, ma. Fred did love him. George was like his father and he loved him. You're damned right about that."

Carefully Agnes tucked away the church program and closed the box, even though she didn't think Harry would be coming home. Harry always spoke about that farm life in rural New York with distain. He had nothing good to say about Agnes's former husband.

In his retirement, Harry intensified his assault on Agnes's social and political positions, which he blamed on bad country upbringing in the North. She seemed driven to equalitarianism, to the common place, in her friends, her politics, and her activism. She enraged him by putting a John Kerry for President bumper sticker on her car and giving money to the Sierra Club and the Union of Concerned Scientists and other such groups that Harry considered contrary to the fundamental principles of America. She became a Unitarian. Harry was a Catholic. He didn't think the Unitarian Church should qualify as a religion since they didn't believe in God. In his opinion, it was just a cover for atheism and a tax-exempt front for liberalism. At social events, she kept her religious, political and social views to herself, and he kept his to himself. They rarely clashed in public. Most of the time they got along and enjoyed their friends, their dinners out, their social circles in the condominium and at the senior lunches. They both grew nervous when with others whose conversation approached contentious topics. They tried to steer the talk to something safe.

With Harry safely in the hospital, she could delve into her past without fear that he would walk in and look over her shoulder. The hospital was assessing the damage from the heart attack today. She was waiting for a phone call about his condition.

The call came in the afternoon. It wasn't Harry who called but Jackie the hospice nurse. She asked that Agnes come to the hospital, but first she put Dr. Hamilton, the cardiologist, on the line.

"We plan to move him to the hospice wing," said Dr. Hamilton. "There we can give him more morphine. We have to cease the other medications, the ones that are keeping his heart functioning. He will not live long with his heart in this condition. When I talked to him about this, he seemed confused. You are his healthcare surrogate. Is it your understanding that this move would be consistent with his wishes?"

"Yes, it is," said Agnes. "He does not want to be kept alive, but I'm still shocked, I thought he had some chance of recovery."

"So did we until we saw the results. He will deteriorate quickly without the medication. When you come to the hospital, go to the hospice wing on the fifth floor. You should come soon."

Outside the room, Jackie met Agnes and told her that Harry was sedated.

"Does he understand?"

"We think so. We told him, not in so many words. He seems lucid. Why don't you go in and talk to him."

It seemed that all Harry Watson's physical imperfections were magnified. The tiny brown spot on his lip looked like a huge coffee stain. The sagging skin around his eyes seemed to drag down his entire face. His hair was unusually thin and void of color, his skin almost translucent with no sign of blood under it. He licked his dry lips with a pale, pink tongue and something inside his mouth clicked when he tried to talk. Even when the words came out, the clicking seemed to obliterate them. All Agnes could hear was the clatter of dry mucous membranes sticking and parting and slapping back together. His right hand was raised and the intravenous tube tugged on his dry skin from underneath the blanket. His skin was purple where the needle went in.

It was hard to believe that underneath what was once a cloak of confidence and determination, a weak heart barely sustained his life. How fragile he really was all along, even when he seemed a powerhouse in his law firm, in court, or at Republican Party organizational meetings. His gray eyes looked sideways at her as if waiting for an answer. Agnes had missed the question.

"What did you say?"

"You must do something."

"What?"

"We need to be together. For eternity. Eternity. We can do this if you become a Catholic. And then the head stone. One stone. For both of us. Side by side in the Catholic cemetery and in heaven. I need you to do this. Father Gillespie will help you."

Agnes looked away. Her mind soared over the valley of years to the dining room of the farmhouse in the Catskill Mountains. When the gun went off that October, she found Fred lying on the floor, blood gathering under his back. George still hadn't realized that the bullet he discharged in the living room went through Fred's abdomen after ripping through the wall. George came running when he heard the screaming. Al and Ethel were already there, and Margaret looked on. Agnes was bending down over Fred. She held his head in her hands and watched blood well up from the left corner of his mouth and grow into a small stream. She tried to believe this was just a wound. Fred knew otherwise.

He asked for a promise—a headstone in the Bloomville cemetery with both their names on it, a violin on her side, a trombone on his. He asked her to promise that she would be buried next to him in the cemetery in Bloomville, where they taught music together for many years and built their home and lives. He asked that someday they would be together again, forever, but he didn't mention heaven, just some generic immortality born of liberal thought. Agnes put her head on his chest and wept.

"Yes. Of course," she said.

Afterward she ordered a modest but fine headstone, just like he asked, with the slide of the trombone crossing the fingerboard of the violin.

Fred's birth and death dates were engraved. Agnes's name was on the stone but the death date was blank. She tried to convince herself that Fred's death was an accident, but in truth she brought him into her home and her life presided over by a crazy, drunken, and dangerous man. She never imagined that her father would become his father and that George would transform her husband into exactly what she didn't want him to be.

Harry knew something was amiss. Agnes's steady gaze out the dark window, her silence, her refusal to look at him were an obvious denial of his request.

"Then just the stone. The two of us. Side by side. Keep your damned religion if that's what you think it is. I don't want to be alone. That's why I married you."

In the face of death, the strength of his personality was waning, and he was afraid, afraid for the next few hours, afraid for eternity. "Damn you," he hissed.

He tried to call out to the nurse, then frantically sought the button that would beep her. Jackie came in after a few minutes.

"Get my lawyer here right now. Richard Malone. Call him. Now. This can't wait. I'm changing my will." He glared at Agnes. "Damn you."

"What's the matter Mr. Watson. Are you feeling OK," Jackie asked calmly. "I'm afraid the office is closed. It's past 8 O'clock. We'll call tomorrow."

"Now! Let me give you his home phone. Three eight three oh hell, what is it? O one eight, I think six. Call him, damn it. Get Father Gillespie here too. The church is getting my money. Father Gillespie will know what to do."

Jackie looked for direction in Agnes's face, but she was frozen in indifference. Jackie walked out, and when she came back, she said, "The nurses have put in a call to Mr. Malone."

Harry seemed to relax. "I don't' want to get upset over this," he said. "Not worth it. My throat hurts. My chest hurts."

Jackie leaned over and patted his right hand. "I'm sorry it hurts," she said. "In a little while we will be along with more morphine. It will feel better."

She motioned Agnes to follow her outside.

"The pain he is describing is a symptom of the heart failing as we have stopped the medication. It's a matter of hours now."

"And the lawyer? He won't make it in time," Agnes said.

"Lawyer?" Jackie asked. "Oh, I haven't heard."

"The priest?"

"The priest was here earlier to do the last rites. We'll take care of all this tomorrow," Jackie said.

Agnes did not stay at the hospital. She went home without saying good-bye to Harry. The next morning, she looked at the answering machine and realized she had slept through a phone call.

ANCESTORS

From what could be gleaned from scant historical records and interviews with oldest family members, Christine's ancestors were good reproducers who led short, miserable lives punctuated by joyful births, exuberant marriages and festive wakes. They began accumulating around the Susquehanna River areas of New York and northern Pennsylvania during the early Twentieth Century. Of the more recent generation, four died of cirrhosis of the liver. Another stumbled out of a bar and stepped into the path of an oncoming car. One was coming home with a puppy, driving down the mountain on icy US 81 toward Binghamton when he skidded under a truck. No one could recall if the puppy, a gift for his children, survived or if a blood alcohol test had been conducted. One uncle hung himself in a barn. Another, Uncle Harry, was an exception to ignoble deaths. He swam to rescue two teenage girls nearly drowning in Lake Ontario. His body was found the next day. The girls survived and told the newspaper they never asked Harry to rescue them. In family discussions, Uncle Harry was revered. As Christine Benson began constructing the family tree, Harry's name was circled but the emphasis was lost in the intricate branches of the family tree that sprawled over the huge chart.

Christine's husband, Bradley Benson, objected to calling the diagram a tree at all, noting the gnarled thread of ancestry lost in a maze of pencil lines. He cited the case of Aunt Lil, who was married to Uncle Frank, the one who hung himself in the barn. He left six children fatherless. After his death his brother, Uncle Martin, married Aunt Lil, then died on the road outside the bar, after begetting four more children. Then a third brother, Uncle Sean, married Aunt Lil and begot three more, ceasing to reproduce only when his liver failed. Aunt Lil continued to reproduce.

"I never saw a tree with branches like that," Bradley said.

One branch of the family tree seemed conspicuously cut off as if by a chainsaw. It was labeled, "Kathleen, lost Aunt Kate."

"This is not a branch but a stump," Bradley said.

"They are my relatives," she said simply, preferring the appearance of harmony to conflict. "You may think it strange that three brothers married the same woman. It may have been an act of kindness from a sense of family responsibility. You are an elitist who is too quick to judge other people's actions."

Now that she had moved to Bloomville in Upstate New York, Christine was determined to learn more about family she had left decades ago, even if the results were not all favorable. Six months after the move, she was still unpacking boxes of her own history while she searched for family records. She had mixed feelings about leaving Long Island for a rural life. She would miss the excitement, the shopping, the vast company she knew living near the city. She would miss her practice in family counseling. But she was two hours away from family members in Binghamton, many of whom she had not met. And the farmhouse she and Bradley bought with a small portion of the money from the sale of their Long Island home was near where Aunt Kate was reported to have landed some 75 years ago when that branch of the family tree tumbled from the trunk.

At the past family reunion in Binghamton, Christine asked about Aunt Kate and got a multitude of responses. She was family legend, but few knew what had become of her or her children or grandchildren, who might still be alive and in the Bloomville area. All agreed that Kathleen was beautiful and thin, with a serpentine body, bouncy red hair, a strawberry complexion and blue eyes like the sky before twilight. She was aloof and impetuous, preferring solitude to the company of family, whom she apparently considered detrimental to her self-concept. She talked of exotic places and rich men. When she left home about six years after finishing high school, she had settled near Bloomville. By one account, she married a doctor. Another had her married to a successful cattle rancher near Cooperstown. Or maybe it was sheep. One relative had heard that she ended up as a bar maid after a drunken husband, maybe not the doctor or the cattle man, divorced her. It was agreed she had several children who likely also had children by now, perhaps many. Her descendants likely were alive and abundant, and Christine was determined to find them and find out what happened to Aunt Kate. It was part of her gift to the family she had not known until now. She would make a family tree and a brief history of the family of Upstate New York, and everyone would get a copy at her expense. She would find the missing Aunt Kate branch and bring together the family. She vowed to complete this project by the next reunion in the coming summer.

She and Bradley spent many hours going through old records in the courthouses of Herkimer and Otsego counties, and in old telephone books in the library looking for traces of Aunt Kate and her offspring. They were unable to find even a marriage record. Without knowing her married name, the search for a death certificate or a birth certificate of her children was futile.

A librarian suggested they look through the cemeteries in the area but did not know of any records to indicate where they all were. Aunt Kate was not in the main Bloomville cemetery, which had a listing of each person interred. Old cemeteries were scattered throughout the hills and woods, along dirt roads and as small islands of headstones in corn fields. Some cemeteries were surrounded by fieldstone fences with wrought-iron gates. Most had a dozen or so graves, some as old as the revolutionary war mixed with others as recent as World War II. Bradley and Christine searched through dozens of such cemeteries without finding a trace of Aunt Kate.

"Maybe we should try the Department of Corrections website for the offspring," Bradley said.

"Who are you to talk," she said. "You'd still be selling securities in New York of you hadn't played with that old man's money."

"It wasn't illegal," he said. "You want to live in Long Island again?"

She had to admit she did not. But she wasn't very happy in the farmhouse either. She silently resented Bradley's slurs on her family and felt overwhelmed by the renovations. She spent the next few weeks aloof from her husband, sometimes sitting with their two dogs, a chocolate lab and a pit bull terrier, or the two cats that came with the farmhouse and quickly took advantage of Christine's compassion by becoming house cats. Christine was a rescuer. You could see it with the animals and before Bradley, apparently, with men.

The rift that was beginning to separate them was quickly repaired when Bradley came home one morning exuberant. He had found something. Christine knew without asking that it had to do with Aunt Kate.

"I have to start from the beginning," he said setting down two cans of paint. "I'm not happy about all of it, but here it is."

It started with a dog. This dog walked along the edge of Henderson Road as if it knew the highway, head bent down against the turbulence of an early north front. The road was empty except for crisp leaves whipped into the wintry air. The flying leaves swirled with the first hints of snow. The dog plodded away from town and toward the remote farm country between Grovesville and Bloomville. It didn't look up as the car neared, as if it knew that in this condition, with the ponderous gate of old age and matted black fur, no one would bother to take it in. Bradley's foot instinctively pulled back from the accelerator. As the car slowed, he looked in the rear view mirror and saw the dog receding.

What could he do? They had two dogs and no room for more, especially an old one with vet bills. Besides, he was focused on his mission right now and there was a sense of urgency. As they remodeled the farmhouse on the outskirts of Bloomville, he and Christine battled over colors. She insisted on the sophisticated hues of new, upscale homes in gated subdivisions of Long Island. He yearned for the simple colors of the country. He knew he was in a skirmish he was destined to lose. She gave him the color swatches, reminding him not to screw up the matt and semigloss.

He found himself watching the dog become a dark, amorphic shape like an oil spot on road. With the distance, Bradley's concern grew and he knew he would have to do something. Christine was compassionate to a fault and would understand his bringing the dog home. Temporarily they could put the dog in the garage or the barn while they put up "found dog" signs; if that didn't work, they would contact the Humane Society to find a place for it. She would agree with him on that plan even though dealing with the dog would interfere with a tight remodeling schedule. He had made up his mind. He would pick up the dog on the way home.

Bradley bought most of his remodeling supplies at Greely's Hardware in Grovesville. He liked dealing with local people more than the corporate robots of The Home Depot or Lowes. He knew Mr. Greely's enthusiastic smile reflected a genuine appreciation for business in the shadow of diminishing income.

"It don't never end," said Mr. Greely when Bradley walked in. "Like a marriage."

"Because of a marriage," Bradley said with a nod.

He handed Mr. Greely the swatches. "A gallon of each. Be sure that sheepskin—no, lamb's wool—is matte and the patina is semigloss. I don't need any further emasculation. Now wait a minute, it might lamb's wool is matte. Oh, damn."

"I'd guess lamb's wool is trim and patina is wall. Most women want semigloss trim and matte wall."

"Well, you know women better than I do."

"I don't know shit about women. I know paint."

At checkout, Mr. Greely dropped the paint cans on the table, and Bradley awaited the weather report.

"Gonna be bitter cold tonight. Snow on the way. Take care on the highway and watch out for deer. They're all over. We need to get more hunters around here."

Bradley waved over his shoulder and walked out of the store on his way to a dog rescue.

He heard a chorus of voices in the sky and looked up to see a chevron of Canadian geese chased by a gray sky. Winter was moving in fast. He accelerated, spun his tires on the new snow and ran a red light as he headed for Henderson Road. He was driving too fast for the snowy conditions and the likelihood of deer, but he didn't have far to go to the site where he saw the dog. As he rounded a curve, a white car parked half way on the road loomed in front of him. Braking and swerving, he just missed hitting it. When the car, a white Toyota convertible, was behind him, he glanced in the rear-view mirror and saw a man and a woman across the road from the car, part way up a six-foot embankment. They were studying a gravestone that was at their eye level. It was in a small cemetery surrounded by a fieldstone fence that had settled into a rock pile. A wrought iron gate hanging by one hinge marked the entrance. The couple were focused on a white stone just inside the gate, in the middle of the opening. Although he had driven this road many times, he had not noticed the cemetery before.

"Strange how history lurks in the natural landscape and emerges in the fall when foliage is gone and trees are bare," he told Christine.

The dog was not where he saw it last.

"You should have picked up the dog the first thing," she told him.

"I was focused on getting the paint you demanded."

"This is my fault?"

"Let me finish."

A few miles down the road he turned around and started looking for the dog, but the road was empty. He rounded the curve where he almost hit the car, and it was gone. Failing to find the dog, he decided to look in the cemetery for Aunt Kate. He found her gravestone at the entrance, the same stone the couple were studying only a few minutes earlier. The stone was about two feet tall, shaped like a house with a pointed roof. It was tilted to the left. Aunt Kate died May 4, 1945.

Christine stared at him for a moment, her mouth open. Then she jumped up and put her arms around his neck. "I can't wait to see it. We'll take a camera. Let's go."

* * *

As Christine photographed the stone, Bradley waited for her excitement to fade to disappointment.

"I guess she never married," Christine said, letting the camera hang from her neck. "We're at another dead end, aren't we? She never changed her name. Her name does not appear anywhere but here."

"This is not really a dead end," said Bradley. "She may have married, changed her name, and changed it back at divorce. She may have lived with a man and had children. She may just have had children. If they were out of wedlock, that could explain why they never reunited with the family.'

"Yes, but it doesn't help us find them." Christine stood up and turned away from the stone.

"We have something you are forgetting—a white Toyota convertible, a Solara. How many convertibles do you think there are around here? They must be relatives."

She nodded.

"Listen, I will find you the people who were at the headstone. I promise. I will do this for you."

As late fall turned to winter, Bradley came to regret his promise. He started asking around town, at Greely's, at the liquor store, at the convenience store, at the bowling alley. No one knew of the car. He put up signs with $100 reward and still no response.

He was painting one day when the phone rang. Mr. Greely called to say there was a white Toyota convertible parked in front of the Lake Country Inn just a few blocks from his store.

* * *

A few old men sat at the bar drinking beer and watching a football game in the dark light. A small fire flickered in the fireplace. An older couple sat at a small table in the corner of the bar. They were eating and talking softly, so intimately that Christine was reluctant to disturb them. She paused for a moment, her husband standing close behind her. Then she walked up to the table, took a deep breath and asked if they owned the Toyota convertible. They did.

She smiled and exhaled as if reaching the end of a long race. "Can I ask you a question?"

"Surely," the man said. He had a round, ruddy face and thin, light hair. His wife's hair was sandy blonde and disheveled. Her eyes sagged.

"We are trying to find a long lost ancestor and you may be able to help us. She is buried in a cemetery and my husband saw you studying her headstone. We hope you might be able to tell us something about the person who was buried under that stone."

The couple looked at each other in amused confusion.

"Sit down," the woman said. "We don't know what you are talking about, but have a seat and we'll try to figure it out."

"Let me explain," said Bradley. "I was driving on Henderson Road a couple months ago, and I saw your car parked on the side of the road by a cemetery. It was on a small hill by the road. The first stone inside the gate is the stone we are referring to—Christine's Aunt Kate. She died in 1945. We believe there are more relatives and maybe you are among them."

The woman shook her head. "I have no idea what you are talking about."

The husband raised his hand. "I know what it is. We were looking for Buford."

"Buford?" Christine said. "Is he her son?"

"Our dog."

"I don't understand," Christine said. "The dog is Buford?"

The man took over. "Our dog left a couple months ago. Someone called to say they saw him on Henderson Road near the cemetery."

Christine took a sharp breath and looked at her husband. She was about to speak when he stopped her with a quick shake of his head. She slowly released the breath intended to fuel her revelation.

As the woman spoke, tears filled her eyes. "He came to our house about eight years ago. He just sat there in the backyard looking at us. He wouldn't come in at first so we fed him outside. After a couple days, he became our house dog. He was a good dog."

When she put her head down, her husband continued. "We don't know where he came from. We don't know what his life was like before he found us. We do know that he was afraid of doors, especially the outside door. We had a hard time coaxing him in. But once inside, he was home. He used to follow me to the barn every day. Oh, and he seemed not to like guns. During hunting season he would hide under the bed when he heard the shots. Anyway, a couple months ago, he disappeared."

His wife wiped her eyes. "Some people tell us dogs run away when they are going to die."

"That's just a story," her husband said. "We don't know that. I think he got spooked by hunters shooting too near the house. Somebody called us and said Buford was walking along Henderson Road. We looked in the cemetery as that was the only cleared area along the road. He couldn't have gotten off the road easily anywhere else because of the growth. He was pretty old. I'm not sure he could even have climbed the hill there. We didn't notice the stone you are talking about."

* * *

The fire in the woodstove had burned low while they were out. Bradley put in more wood. Christine sat on the floor surrounded by piles of papers, photographs, file folders, and the genealogical chart of her family.

"I guess I'll read," he said and went upstairs. Later he smelled an acrid odor coming from downstairs. He went back down to see what was burning. Christine stood over the open wood stove, feeding it with papers. The piles of papers and photographs were gone and in their place was a small wooden box. As she fed more papers into the wood stove, she didn't acknowledge his presence. He looked into the stove and saw photographs and papers burning. The genealogical chart was consumed in seconds. A photograph of Christine in her graduation cap and gown at Columbia University was curling and turning black at the edges. "What the hell are you doing? This is a story of your life you are burning."

"It may be the story of a life," she said, "but it will all fit in a box."

Bradley put on his coat and walked outside. Light snowflakes were falling in the yard, coming to rest on the bare branches of maple trees, forming white cones on a few apples that still hung from the branches, and on red sumacs along the driveway. The rough edges of fieldstone walls were rounded and softened by a layer of snow. Two trails of footprints leading to the house were slowly filling in and in a few hours would be gone. Smoke from the brick chimney rose straight into a windless sky.

FIELD OF STONES

Something about the way Dr. Martin Williams reached into the plastic bowl jarred memories that tumbled into Lawrence Parker's mind, blocking the white light of the examining room. Parker remembered his mother standing by the green linoleum breakfast bar with a blue bowl of oatmeal that she stirred methodically. The more she stirred it, the greater the chance that each of three children would get the same number of raisins. When it was served, Larry stirred through his portion pretending to be picky but silently counting raisins. A flood of unwelcomed childhood follies followed. In high school band, he played first trumpet and sat directly across from Myrtle Miller, who played first clarinet. Each day at band practice, he looked past his sheet music, past the bobbing hands of the conductor, who was his father. There he could see the clarinet mouthpiece clenched securely in Myrtle Miller's soft, fleshy lips, the black instrument at a downward angle through the gully of her new breasts, discharging music that swirled between her milky knees and into the secret darkness of her skirt.

Every morning, his father would tap the music stand to get everyone's attention, but Larry Parker was lost in the twilight that receded between Myrtle's thighs. One day Larry found himself staring at an empty chair, and it stayed empty for a long time, long after it was generally acknowledged by students and teachers that Myrtle was gone. His father did not fill the chair out of respect for Mr. and Mrs. Miller, a humble, God-fearing couple who attended all services at the Methodist Church and all high school events intended for parents, where they spoke softly and appropriately and offended no one. They were proud to have given their daughter a traditional name that reflected their hopes for a traditional life. They did everything right, Larry's parents said. They did not deserve this.

When Myrtle disappeared, Larry lost a delicious fantasy that had started his school days. He remembered Mr. and Mrs. Miller's faces after their first tragedy carved their joint visages into stony portraits. He knew there was something there he could not comprehend. Years later, after meeting dozens of survivors of senseless crimes, he thought he understood the pain of parents losing a child. And now, losing a second. Was it worse to lose a child and not know what happened or to lose one and know? How much worse would it be if they knew that Floyd Miller's had been beaten beyond recognition and the task of identifying him involved trying to find some teeth.

Dr. Martin Williams pushed the horn-rimmed, magnifying glasses to the top of his head and peeled off his latex gloves.

"I don't get it," he said, setting down the bowl. "The guy had 16 in the maxilla and 16 in the mandible and I can only find a few tooth fragments. There are quite a few bone fragments, but what happened to rest of the guy's teeth? There are no fillings in the pieces we have here."

"I'd bet dollars to donuts he didn't have 32 teeth left," his assistant, Thornton Hartley, said. "I'd have guessed from what I heard about the people out there, he may not have had teeth. Not that a guy with poor dental hygiene deserves to have his brains bashed in. But this is a case of woodchuck justice. You can't expect a clean case from woodchuck justice." He swiveled his chair 180 degrees and picked up a newspaper. "We don't even know if he had a dentist."

Lt. Lawrence Parker was stunned by this indifference and worried about the lack of identification. "The DA is meeting with the killer and his public defender tomorrow hoping for a second-degree murder plea. He wants a positive identification for the record. DNA tests are going to take over a week. Obviously facial identification is out of the question."

"We'll try an X-ray of the—skull," said Williams. Hartley shook his head while Williams disappeared into the X-ray room. When he returned with the film, they stared at the screen. Then Williams and Hartley agreed there was no useful evidence in the bowl or in the X-ray.

"A couple of these teeth might serve to identify him if we could find his dentist, but generally they look for fillings," Hartley said on the way back to his desk. "Who found this guy? Can't they do an ID based on clothing?"

"I'm still working on the scenario," Parker said.

"Who the hell processed this crime scene? Either they missed some evidence or this guy's been living on soup," Hartley said as he scanned the newspaper.

"Our crime scene people did it," Parker said.

"Well maybe you should give it another look," Hartley said.

"It's been returned to the occupants," Parker said. "I have an interview there with the guy's stepdaughter and another one after that."

"Well there's nothing here to tell us who this John Doe was," Hartley said.

Williams was more respectful but no more optimistic. "He's right. I'm sorry. We have nothing in the way of evidence here."

Parker was sorry too, sorry for the parents of Floyd and Myrtle Miller. Parker and Myrtle Miller were classmates when Myrtle disappeared in her senior year.

After that, the parents were seen only at church and they usually left with barely a word. When Floyd was baptized a year later, the church hosted a brief social after the service the welcome to new arrival. Thirty years later, when Floyd was killed, Mr. and Mrs. Miller were in their 70s. Parker returned to his hometown to investigate the killing. The visit was the first since he left home for college. He went to the home of Mr. and Mrs. Miller with a phlebotomist to obtain blood samples for DNA identification of Floyd's remains. Mr. and Mrs. Miller did not know what DNA was, but they submitted quietly.

Parker was preparing to interview Floyd's stepdaughter, Tina, as part of the investigation. A couple years ago, Floyd married Elsie Cramer—an older woman and Tina's mother—and adopted Tina and her brother, Billie, when her two children were in their late-teens. A few months before the murder, Elsie Cramer died. Tina had lost a mother and an adoptive father. Her brother, Billie, also was killed. His body was found next to Floyd Miller's. Both died from shotgun blasts, but Floyd—the apparent target of the violence—was savagely beaten.

* * *

The Reverend Florence Willoughby was proud of the sermon she had prepared to stimulate a congregation that she sensed had grown sleepy, or maybe, she mused, were born sleepy. She spent weeks watching vampire shows on television, reading about vampires in magazines and looking up scripture about how souls were saved by the spilling of innocent blood. She decided to give her congregation a combination of shock and contemporary relevance. On that Sunday morning she arrived with barely a minute to spare. She worried that in her haste she would falter while presenting the sermon. Mrs. Jaquays, her scarecrow frame struggling to keep up, followed The Reverend Willoughby to the altar. She tried her best to talk to the pastor, but Florence waved her away. "After the service," she said, the black robe flowing in wind of her gait. She mounted the purple, carpeted steps, turned at the pulpit, put on her glasses, and looked up over them to the congregation.

She was aware that her congregation was unusually solemn. She was also aware that she was not an attractive figure standing on the stage of her weekly performance. Her black robe did not hide her pudgy middle. She hoped her plainness would help the congregation relate to her. During communion she put special emphasis on blood. It was a prelude to the sermon. "This is the blood of Christ. It has been shed for you and for many. Drink in remembrance of me."

To begin her sermon, she explained the importance of relevance, then got right to vampires in the media. In a TV series, an invention called *True Blood* has made it possible for vampires to come out of their coffins and live among humans. As they struggle for recognition, anti-vampire groups are formed.

"We have a bumper crop of vampires created by the likes of Anne Rice and Stephenie Meyer, whose *Twilight* series ignited vampire mania. The blood-thirsty, blood-sucking demons have become the idols of our youths. Meanwhile, their parents are notorious 'hemophobics.' Just the mention of *blood* makes them queasy."

Yes, she thought, they seemed queasy about the topic. She could feel it in the purple ambience. So much the better. Shock them with relevance. She plodded on.

"When was the last time we sang, *There is a Fountain Filled with Blood* or *Power in the Blood*? *Alas and Did My Savior Bleed*? How about *Oh the Blood will Never Lose its Power*? *Redeemed by the Blood of the Lamb*? *Nothing but the Blood*? Anybody heard of these? Look in the index of your Bible. Do you see an entry for blood? No? Now look in the TV guide. We are awash in a sea of blood, yet is anyone saved by it?

"Vampires offer eternal life and damnation in exchange for souls. They require blood sacrifices while our instrument of salvation and eternal life—the blood of Jesus—is shrouded in secrecy. Jesus said to experience salvation and eternal life we must drink his blood. Yes, salvation comes at a price, my Christian friends—the sacrifice of innocent blood. Jesus paid this price for us.

"How many of you invited the blood of damnation into your homes?" The congregation was silent. "How many of you asked to have the blood of salvation in your homes?" The congregation remained silent, but the Reverend Willoughby could detect nervous motions in some of the congregation. "Well, we may get what we ask for and we will get what we deserve."

She chanted, "What can wash away my sins? Nothing but the blood of Jesus. What can make me whole again? Nothing but the blood of Jesus." She chanted the questions again, then beckoned to the audience to respond. They did not. Something was wrong. She saw Mr. and Mrs. Miller in the front row. Mr. Miller looked solemn. His head wagged from side to side, his baleful eyes were fixed on the altar. Mrs. Miller was crying. After the benediction, the Millers left quickly. When some members of the congregation explained to The Reverend Willoughby what had happened to Floyd Miller, she turned pale, sat down and put her head in her hands. She wept, prayed, and wished she had chosen a different sermon. Then she wished Floyd Miller had not been killed.

* * *

Fall was settling into the valley. Lt. Lawrence Parker could see the signs of it before he left town—snow blowers and log splitters were displayed in front of Lowes. Hunters were buying ammo at Wal-Mart. Every kind of store sported outdoor displays of pumpkins and dried corn stalks. The sherbet pastels of fall leaves washed over the forests along the back roads to Bloomville. Amish farmers stacked firewood for sale in front of their farms and harvested oats in brown mounds. Draft horses pulled old hay balers, and Amish children sold vegetables at roadside stands.

The Amish farms reminded him of the farms of his childhood, but Amish farmers were a different lot. It seemed that all Amish family members pitched in seven days a week to manage the farm. Some farmers he remembered received their weekly milk checks and headed for the taverns, coming home penniless days later, hoping their kids kept the farm going. Elsie Cramer grew up on one of those farms.

Parker arrived at the house where Floyd and his family had lived. Tina still lived there with her young son. Two maple trees in front of the tiny brown house had yellow plastic tape around the trunks, as if the family placed yellow ribbons to beckon Floyd home. A rusty, blue Neon was overturned, its tires raised in the air like paws of a dead animal. Parker stepped around a minefield of dog crap and pulled open the wooden screen door to knock on the inside door. One hinge broke and the door hung on the lower hinge. There was no doorbell. A dog barked inside, and a woman barked back. When the woman opened the door, she blew smoke and flicked the end of cigarette out the door. Parker introduced himself.

Tina looked at the screen door hanging on one hinge. "You trying to break in?"

"No mam. I knocked. Are you Tina?"

Two plump breasts wiggled beneath a half-opened blouse. "Well that's what it says," she said, looking down to the top of the left breast, where a tattoo spelled her name. She had tattoos on both arms that were so elaborate Parker did not try to decipher them. She seemed to have barely cleared being a teenager.

Tina dragged a skinny dog out of the room and closed the door. She turned off the television, sat on the sofa, and leaned over a coffee table cluttered with dirty dishes and silverware. She lit a cigarette and used a bowl of soggy Cheerios and milk to put out the ashes. The room smelled of smoke, mold and dog urine.

"Miss Miller, I am doing the investigation on Floyd Miller and need some more information. I'm the man you talked to when you called the police." She puckered up her mouth and mashed the cigarette into the Cheerios with a hiss. "I need to talk about your mother and stepfather."

Parker took out a small notebook.

"My mother's dead," she said.

"Yes. We understand that some activities back then may have led up to the murders. Can you tell me about your mother?"

Elsie Cramer was born to run, and by all accounts, even those of her daughter, she was in a perpetual marathon of drinking and chasing men. Her early marriage to Kyle Cramer lasted long enough to produce two children, Billie and Tina, but not long enough for them to get to know their father. Elsie was pretty once, by the pictures Tina showed Parker, but by middle age, she was washed out. That's when Floyd Miller came along. He loved her and wanted to marry her but had no regular job. He had just returned from Iraq with an injury and got his discharge. Elsie figured a man needed to have a way to support a woman with two kids and a drinking habit. So Floyd went to school on the GI bill and became a plumber. He also worked when he could as a substitute school bus driver. He was careful not to take the pain medication for the war injury when he drove the school bus. He and Elsie married a few years ago. Tina considered Floyd her father because he loved her and adopted her and Billie, with the blessing of Kyle Cramer. Kyle was not allowed much time with his kids even when they were young.

Billie, with Elsie's help, had obtained credit cards in Floyd's and Elsie's names, and took out cash advances. After Elsie died, Floyd found out about the credit cards.

"That's when all this shit started," Tina said. "Floyd was real pissed off. He owed more than $20,000 and had nothing for it. Billie was real pissed off because Floyd cut him off and he couldn't get any more money. Then it got worse. Billie was running with some drug guys from the valley. He and this guy named Don that everyone called Axel come and asked Floyd for money. Billie said Floyd was his father and was responsible for giving him money. Billie laughed at Floyd, laughed right in his face. When Billie and Axel left, Billie asked me where Floyd kept the pain drugs. I didn't know."

A boy wandered into the room, walked toward Tina, and hid behind her, nuzzling his face into the space between her neck and shoulder. Parker greeted him with a "hello son" but he knew that would not appeal to a kid these days. He didn't know what to say. Neither did the kid.

"Your son?"

"Yep. Justin."

"How old are you?"

"Me? Oh I know what you are getting at," she said. "Yep, I had him young. He's a good boy. Just his teacher didn't like him sharing that stuff about Floyd and Billie."

"About the murders?"

Tina explained that she went to the stock car races the Sunday of the killing and planned to come back late that afternoon. She left Justin with a neighbor. After the races, Billie called and told her not to go to the house that day. He said Axel was coming for Floyd. Tina called the neighbor and asked if Justin could spend the night. The next morning, Justin went to the house alone to dress for school. It wasn't until the kindergarten kids got to share that Justin said something about the two dead men in the house.

"So Justin found them?"

"Yep, and the teacher called me and I called the police because I figured what had happened and that Axel did it."

Parker focused on the boy.

"Justin. Did you take anything from the house besides the clothes for school?"

Justin wrapped his arms around his mother's leg and did not answer.

Parker gave up on Justin and addressed Tina. "Did Floyd have a dentist?"

"Not that I know of."

* * *

In the darkness of hands cupped over wet eyes, Florence Willoughby saw clearly, and she was troubled by what she saw. Her masterpiece sermon was not about the follies of vampire mania, the presence of blood-fearing Christians or the importance of salvation by sacrifice. It was about vanity—her own. She had planned to wake up a sleepy congregation with her vast knowledge, her extensive religious research, her dramatic delivery, and she failed because she was ignorant of the people in her congregation. She knew the names and the faces but not the people. As an outsider, she would never know the lives of the people of Bloomville. But she could make amends, and the place to start was the Bloomville Country Store, just across the street from the Methodist Church. The bread and eggs she bought were an excuse to start a conversation with three old men who sat at the coffee bar. She heard the conversation about Floyd Miller's murder dwindle as she walked in. Teddy Herndon, a rough, aging farmer, once a lecher, changed the subject.

"Sorry I missed the service today, Miss Willoughby," he said, tipping an imaginary hat.

"You miss the service every Sunday, Teddy."

"My wife come," he said.

"That doesn't count." She looked at the other two men who she guessed were trying to be invisible, also having missed church. Martin Owen had an excuse because he was Catholic. "Well I have a chance for you to make it up. We're going to get a headstone for Floyd Miller, a very nice one. Since you missed dropping money in the collection plate, you can contribute here. Floyd was a good man. His parents are good people."

The three men turned to one another and nodded in agreement, smiling at the chance to agree with a minister whose services they did not attend.

"Damned right, he was a good man, Miss Willoughby," Martin Owen chimed in. He was a ruddy faced Irishman who employed Floyd part-time before Floyd became a plumber. "He worked hard to keep Elsie and her kids in food and clothes."

George Allen was a retired school teacher whose granddaughter rode Floyd's bus occasionally. He told Ms. Willoughby that the kids horsed around on Floyd because they knew he was a softie and he liked them. "He never got mad about it," George said. "He just grinned. I think he loved the kids. It was like he was a kid himself when he drove the bus."

George Allen remembered Floyd's sister, Myrtle, from years ago. "Tough on the old couple to lose two kids, to outlive them both. Myrtle was a very pretty girl who got running with the wrong crowd. Some guys from the valley. Used to come up and take her out in a convertible, and one day she didn't come home. She was a lot better student than Floyd, just too pretty for her own good."

Teddy cast a sidelong glance at George. "Can't you say nothing nice about Floyd?"

"I have."

"Well you said he wasn't a good student, like he was dumb or something. I heard you. You should have more respect now that he's dead."

"I never said that. Christ, Teddy, you don't even make sense."

The conversation erupted into a chorus of accusations and denials. "I didn't say that," George said when the ruckus settled. "I didn't say that at all."

Martin Owen waited for his chance. "I warned him a few years ago. We were having coffee at the bowling alley. I said 'you're better off a single man.' You couldn't tell him anything."

"A man's got two brains," said George Allen, "an upper one and a lower one. The lower one is not real bright, but it calls a lot of shots."

"See," said Teddy Herndon. "There you go again."

"I'm not referring to his upper brain."

"Okay, Okay," Florence said. "We can agree Floyd was a good man and deserves a good memorial. His parents deserve it for their son."

She extracted promises of $20 from each one, to be paid when the account was set up. After she left, Martin Owen noticed a bag on the counter. It contained bread and eggs. He looked at his two friends. "Women preachers. Won't see that in the Catholic Church."

* * *

Kyle Cramer was a massive specimen of a farm boy who set a record for throwing a bale of hay and reportedly could open beer bottles with his teeth. With shoulders and biceps like Virginia hams, a flat top crew cut with some gouges on the side, he was a formidable example of force, but he was deemed unreliable for the six-man football team. Kyle flunked English the first semester of his senior year and bullied Larry Parker, maybe lashing out because Parker was a teacher's kid. Parker inflamed the resentment by boasting that he was going to a top-notch college. In limited discourse with Kyle Cramer, Larry Parker implied that brains would win out over brawn. The test came when Larry was walking to his locker and Kyle tripped him. As

Larry rose to his feet, he grabbed the bottom of Kyle's sweater and pulled it up and over his head. Then he planted a fist in the middle of the cloth ball that rested on Kyle's shoulders. Kyle tore the sweater from around his head and discharged a guttural sound. Larry remembered nothing after that until he looked up and saw some students and a couple teachers standing over him. The side of his head throbbed so bad he felt he would throw up. That afternoon in detention, he and Kyle sat at opposite ends of a table, Parker's one eye swollen shut, his other watching Kyle rub his bruised nose.

The trip to Bloomville brought back old resentments and fears. Parker admitted to himself that getting beat up by Kyle Cramer was one reason he went into law enforcement. He would be wearing a gun and badge the next time he encountered a man like Kyle Cramer. Today he would interview Kyle because his son, Billie, was dead along with Floyd Miller. Parker did not expect to gain much information from the interview. He was eager to see how Kyle would react to the uniform, the badge, and the gun. When he got out of the car, he stood next to the State Police insignia, his right hand resting on his holster. He did not recognize Kyle Cramer's face, but the build was unmistakable. Kyle leaned into the lawn mower with arms that could lift four lawnmowers. When Kyle saw the police car, he stopped the lawnmower and walked over. He recognized Parker immediately and didn't glance at the gun or badge. He extended a massive hand. A smile curled on his weathered face.

"Kyle, I am sure you know why I'm here."

"Hi, Larry."

"Lawrence."

"Lawrence. I expect you saw the flier about the cat."

"No. The cat? No."

Kyle's wife, Chrissy, joined them and Kyle introduced Parker as a former schoolmate. Then they talked about the cat. She was a house cat, kind of young, that was given to them. Chrissy left the door open to chase out a red squirrel, and the cat followed it out the door. They've been looking for her for four days, putting up fliers, and making phone calls.

"I came to talk about your son and the murder of Floyd Miller. You must know your son, Billie, is dead."

"Real sorry about that. Floyd was a good man. My boy Billie, he was not good most of his life. We tried to warn Floyd—warn him about Elsie and Billie. I lost my son three times. Once when me and Elsie split up. Then again when he started running with those druggies down in the valley. And now he's dead along with Floyd. Tina's a good girl. I only lost her once. Then we lost the cat."

Chrissy jumped into the conversation. One day Billie came to talk to them. He brought a friend from the valley named Axel. Billie told them he was proud to be Kyle's son and Chrissy's stepson, even though Floyd adopted him. While they were talking, Axel wandered around the house. A few days later, Chrissy found out that their credit cards were gone. "We were $8,000 in the hole," she said. "We called Billie and he said to talk to Axel."

Kyle Cramer nodded in agreement. "I told that boy, I said the farther your ass is from me, the better. And he says, 'how dare you say that of your own flesh and blood.' I tell him, I know flesh and blood, and I know bones and he's bad to bone. Then I heard maybe he tried to save Floyd."

"He did," Parker said. "We think he went there when he knew Floyd was in danger. We don't know what happened. Maybe in the end he was a hero."

"I don't know about a hero. I'm glad he did right in the end. I'm proud of him for that. Things have been changing fast around here. Drugs are coming in and people are getting killed. Back when we were young, you'd get in trouble for having a six-pack or getting into a fight. That was considered bad. You remember that fight we had? We got detention for it."

Parker pretended to have forgotten. "Yes, I do remember now that you mention it."

"My nose hurt for weeks. I never messed with you again. I learned something then—respect. You have to respect people. Now we got these outsiders coming in like that guy Axel. The respect is gone. It's not like it used to be around here."

Lawrence Parker felt ashamed that he harbored resentment about the fight, while Kyle Cramer learned respect from it. Parker wished he had left his badge, gun, and uniform in the car.

Kyle Cramer took a few papers from his wife and handed them to Parker. "She's a calico cat," he said. "They used to say that if a cat doesn't come back in a week, it's gone. We never had coyotes before. Now they say three days, maybe less because of the coyotes. We aren't giving up yet. If you can help me out with some of these fliers...."

* * *

Over winter and spring, no one in Bloomville killed anyone or did any other serious misdeed, as far as the law knew. Lawrence Parker wrapped up his work in the town where he grew up and packed away the memories this brief reunion had dredged up. Don "Axel" Drummond was serving 25 years for second-degree murder. Floyd Miller's tombstone had been installed under the supervision of The Reverend Florence Willoughby and Floyd's survivors. Lawrence had not seen it but had heard it was elegant. Lawrence kept a note from Kyle Cramer on the cork board by his desk. The note stated that Kyle was pleased to see is old classmate and that the calico cat had come home after nearly a month.

Summer in Bloomville was off to a good start. The days leading up to the summer solstice were gloriously and clear, with cool, starry skies at night, although afternoon and evening thunderstorms were common. "God knows we need the rain," said Evelyn Herndon, Teddy's wife. With ideal water and sun, the corn was coming along nicely. "Corn knee high by the Fourth of July," Teddy Herndon said with pride and optimism. Kids on summer vacation brought home their limit of trout from the creek. The first farmer's market ever in Bloomville opened in the park on Thursdays, with a great supply of Amish vegetables and jams. Because of the frequent late showers, no one was surprised when rain and thunderstorms were forecast for a Saturday night. It was the night before the Methodist Church's ice cream social. Residents went to sleep expecting a brief rainstorm and awoke to find the power out and the creek roaring, swollen with rain water gathered from the hills and tributaries. The flooding was a disaster unlike any the oldest people in town could remember. Three cars floated into the school soccer field. Others were overturned in the park hundreds of feet from where they had been parked. Rusty fuel tanks floated out of the ground and came to rest on sidewalks or lawns. Boulders, logs, and parts of houses and sheds washed in piles in grassy parks. Asphalt was peel off the roads like cheap linoleum flooring. Basements were flooded and filled with mud. Furnaces, washers, dryers, water heaters were destroyed. The smell of fuel oil was in the air and the mud was covered with a rainbow sheen of petroleum. The village's only main road was transformed into a river. The rain had stopped by morning, and stunned residents stood in the mud contemplating their losses.

The Methodist Church was on high ground on the north side of the main road. Tables and chairs set up the night before for the ice cream social were wet. Some church volunteers arrived from the hill on the north side and discussed what to do about the ice cream social, considering the freezer was not freezing. Mrs. Jaquays decided to start the ice cream social early before the ice cream melted. She told everyone to bring their frozen food and the church would cook it on the propane grill for displaced residents. By late morning several dozen wet and weary people had gathered in front of the church. They watched the parade of garbage—plastic containers, propane tanks, porches, floating down the road as the flood diminished.

Suddenly a bedraggled naked woman ran past the church, her bare feet splashing in the muddy water. She was roundish and pudgy, like cooking oil in a plastic bag, her breasts and belly flopping with each step. Her long dark hair was twisted against her wet skin, white as the belly of a fish.

Teddy Herndon's eyes followed her. "Well Jesus Christ," he said, forgetting he was in the company of church goers. "She ain't pretty but she is naked."

"For God's sake," said Mrs. Jaquays, putting her hands up to her tightly gathered gray hair. "Someone help her."

Several residents ran to her while others pulled blankets and towels out of the church. The woman resisted but was exhausted and soon she was wrapped and lying on the church floor. While the residents waited for an ambulance, Mrs. Jaquays and a few others tried to talk to her, but the woman responded only with low guttural growls. Her dark eyes shifted back and forth in panicked motion. After a while she slept. People who gathered in front of the church seemed confused. No one knew who she was or where she came from or why she was running down the road naked, an event as unique in Bloomville as the flood.

Two paramedics arrived an hour later with a stretcher. They asked for help in carrying the woman to the ambulance, which could not get near the village because of the flood waters. George Allen and Teddy Herndon volunteered. When they returned, they were stunned at the size of the crowd. Residents with shovels, wheel barrows, and hand carts were preparing to help people remove mud and debris from the basements of flood victims. An Amish horse and wagon waited a short way off. Some church women led by The Reverend Florence Willoughby were interviewing residents to try to assign work crews based on need. The ice cream social table was covered with food, and several men were cooking on the church grill. Mrs. Jaquays looked up at the weary volunteers and grinned, waving her boney hands to show the extent of the food. "We've got more food than you can shake a stick at," she said.

Lt. Lawrence Parker missed the ice cream social but arrived in time to interview a few stragglers about the mysterious woman. She was Jane Doe, identification unknown. Parker called the medical examiner to make sure DNA testing was in progress.

"It's not likely to produce anything, if she is from that area," Dr. Martin Williams told him. "We have only three DNA samples on file from Bloomville."

* * *

Mr. Miller answered the door. Lt. Lawrence Parker and a female investigator—Marge Stratford—stood on the porch steps. Parker handed Mr. Miller the search warrant. Mrs. Miller stood behind her husband, as if he protected her.

"Mr. and Mrs. Miller, this is a search warrant. We are going to search your house with an order from the court. Do you understand what that means?"

"Please," she whimpered.

"We are very old," said Mr. Miller.

"I know," Parker said, "but we have to do our job."

In the basement, they found the bomb shelter, built in the 1950s during the Cuban missile crisis and reworked into a cell. The heavy door was bolted from without. A fold-away bed with a muddy mattress was against one wall. The walls were decorated with paintings of Jesus. A picture of a boy—probably Floyd Miller—was on a tall dresser.

During the flood, water had covered the bed and now six inches of mud covered the floor.

Parker read Mr. and Mrs. Miller their rights and explained the kidnapping charges. Marge took out the handcuffs, but on a glance from Parker put them behind her back. "It's protocol," she said but did not press the issue.

"Can you help us, Mr. Parker?" Mr. Miller pleaded. "Myrtle played in your father's band."

"I can try to help Myrtle. But you'll need a lawyer to help you. I'm sorry."

When they were seated in the back of the car, Parker took a roll of crime scene tape and wrapped it around the house.

* * *

Lt. Lawrence Parker was not on patrol, so he wore civilian clothes to work. The ground was still soggy outside the State Police office, but the place was drying out. The sun was bright, and through the window Parker could see the leaves teased to motion by a gentle breeze. He realized that although he investigated people as perpetrators and victims, he never touched the nerves, the flesh, the meanings of their lives. He couldn't imagine what Myrtle Miller endured those many years in captivity or what Kyle Cramer endured in losing a son three times. Or what those thirty days were like when his cat was missing.

He visited Myrtle Miller in the hospital that morning. She was under psychiatric care and had not yet spoken or shown any sign of recognizing people. He stood for a few moments over her bed, then touched her forehead. Her face was white and puffy, her eyes nearly closed. Although she seemed unaware of him, he wanted to say something touching. Nothing came to mind. He said aloud, "Good bye, Myrtle." He left and drove to Bloomville to find Floyd Miller's grave.

Knowing only that the headstone was new, he was not sure how he would recognize it from a distance. The cemetery he remembered from years ago was small, with old stones covered by lichens. Now it had grown to a field of stones, new and glossy ones with fancy lettering sprinkled among the dark and weathered monuments. At the far end of the new section of the cemetery near a line of trees, he saw a middle aged man and woman with two children trying to move a fallen tree from a grave site. The ground was raised in front of the stone and the grass was rich green. Parker stepped up to help with the tree removal, and with some effort, they pushed the trunk aside. Floyd Miller's name was on the polished stone. A cross adorned a pastoral scene. Under it were the words, "Blessed are the pure in heart, for they shall see God." *Matthew 5:8.*

The man wiped his hands, then extended a hand to Parker.

"I'm Floyd's cousin."

"Well, not really his cousin, not anymore," his wife corrected. "Really you're his—"

"He's always going to be my cousin. Name is Andy and this is my wife, Mary Jo."

"Sorry about what happened to Floyd," said Parker. "I figure he was a real good guy." Realizing he was trying sound like one the town folk, he turned away and looked at stone.

"Yes he was," Andy said. "I don't think I know you."

"No," said Parker. "I don't think you do."

MARGARET'S ROOM

She was about eight years old when she left the house on Erickson Street. At that time she did not understand the questions of finances and mortgages, only that her father had died and that his death was remotely connected to their leaving. Almost from the day she left she had forgotten her room. That forgetting was cruel, as cruel as leaving and forgetting an intimate childhood friend. It was thoughtless, as children are thoughtless. But Margaret had forgotten her room.

It was bitter cold in Rochester, New York, in February. At the bus stop, she fumbled for the change but could not pick it up because of her gloved hand. She took off her glove and noticed her naked hand, brown, thin and bony. The fingers were long, with thick knuckles and wrinkled skin. Her hand trembled. It was only slightly easier to handle the money with her bare fingers.

When she paid the fare she hastened to put on the glove again. She sat down nervously in a seat near the front. There were only a few bundled-up people on the bus, and this made the sense of cold deepen.

How would she ask the people in the Erickson Street house if she could enter and see her room?

For the past few years Margaret received unwelcomed signals of her ailing mind. They visited her at various times of the day in many different places—misplaced items, forgotten names, unfinished sentences and thoughts. But she was now amazed at—and very pleased by—how easily her mind soared over the great valley of years, and with never a thought of the room from the moment she left the house until now. The memory was fresh and crisp.

This room was not her bedroom but a playroom. It was a bright room with a large window capturing sunlight, projecting a gentle shaft of yellow light over an oriental rug and onto the flower pattern of the wall. Next to the window was a rocker. Margaret never sat in the rocker for that place was always occupied by a large ceramic doll with a soft white face and a billowy dress. When Margaret touched the rocker, the doll rocked for hours.

She would sit on a rug in the middle of the room and look out the window. In the center of the window view was a large, green maple tree. A rose garden framed in fieldstone was arranged around the tree in a "U" shape that opened toward the window, toward Margaret. Sometimes snow lay in graceful folds over the contour of the land, as if someone had shaken out a sheet and let it fall over the roses and grass. The snow sparkled, the rain hissed, the moon cast shadows over grass, snow, roses, and bare bushes.

On a table near the far wall was a game. It resembled a chess game, but instead of chess pieces it had peculiar animal figures carved of dark wood. She didn't know how the game was played nor did she touch a single piece. The game was already in progress at the early fringes of Margaret's memory, but the positions of the pieces didn't change from then on, and she knew where each one was.

A piano was in the room. Margaret began playing piano at a classmate's house and took informal instruction from her classmate's mother because her parents could not afford regular lessons. She regularly visited her friend to practice, but the real composition took place in her room, where she enjoyed solitude. Sometimes she spent hours playing, pushing white keys and black keys and listening to the results. Initially what came out was undeniably ugly, even to its untrained author. But after a time she composed pretty pieces that she played while the doll listened. She refined them at her friend's house and play them for her friend's mother, who loved them.

Margaret particularly liked one song. It was about the doll's life, her growing up, having a family. It was a sweet song with many deep and warm chords. Often she would give the rocking chair a push and sit down to play. When she finished, the chair was still rocking, the doll looking steadily at her with soft, blue eyes.

When Margaret was still very young—she could not recall exactly what age—she discovered something unusual about her room. Her mother and father would be at work. She and the maid, Hilda, would be alone in the house, and Hilda sometimes could not find her.

Several times Margaret calmly emerged from her room and walked into the living room. Upon seeing her, Hilda grabbed her up hysterically, wailing about her dear, lost child. Hilda was of less than average intelligence, and Margaret sensed this. Hilda would recite the places she had looked for Margaret—half of them outside, and all of them unlikely—and then she would ask Margaret where she had been.

Margaret would simply mention a place that was not on the list. The next time, the revised list would include the previous alleged hiding place, but there were always enough unmentioned places in the big house on Erickson Street to keep her out of trouble. She was very pleased with herself for this secret and never imagined that there would be serious problems because of it. But one Sunday while walking home from church her father broached the subject.

"You know, Margaret," he said, growing stern, "your mother and I wanted to talk to you about a problem." Margaret deliberately looked horrified. "No, no, it's not a big problem. It's really just a little problem."

"Well?" She laughed silently. She had sabotaged the introduction.

"Well, some neighbors have told us that you leave the house now and then and run off for hours. We'd like to know where you go, and we'd like to know why you sneak out like that. Hilda is worried sick."

Margaret was confused and angry. "I don't sneak out of the house."

The firmness of her voice should have ended the conversation. She was not a great liar, although she could lie if she had to. When the truth was on her side, she was very strong, and she hadn't left the house.

"Now Margaret," her mother began with no more basis and even less direction than her father, "you know we always believe you because we know our little girl does not lie. But if you lie now we'll never believe you again. Now why don't you tell us the truth?"

"I never leave the house. Who told you? Mrs. Butler?"

"No."

"Mrs. Kirkpatrick?"

"No."

"Well, they're our neighbors."

"No dear, not those neighbors."

"Hilda. I bet it was Hilda."

"All we're trying to do is find out where you go and of course why you go, and we're trying to stop you from going again because we worry about you. The cars go very fast now and children are sometimes killed on the roads. Do you want to die?"

She was pensive a moment. What did it mean to die? "No."

Her parents looked at each other and silently agreed to drop the topic. She knew they would discuss it with Hilda later.

Margaret was surprised, then perplexed, then concerned when thinking back over the times she had spent in the room she realized that she was the only person who had entered. Indeed that was the most important aspect of the room. She had considered telling her friends about the room or just mentioning it to her parents, but after the Sunday morning discussion she knew that it was a private place. In fact she would have to actively keep it private if she intended to preserve the intimate character of the room. And if one of her parents barged in while she was playing the piano or contemplating the green maple tree and asked her to take her medicine or brush her teeth or eat her supper of liver and onions, the charm of the room would be lost.

She imagined the horrible look that would streak her own face, the sudden stillness of the rocker, the silence of the piano. Her parents would pack up the animal pieces on the chessboard. They would wash the curtains, sweep the room, shake out the rug and rearrange the furniture. And maybe even lock the door.

One cold, rainy evening in the springtime of one very memorable year, her parents sat listening to the news on the radio. There was a war in Europe and it was getting bad. Her parents were worried and agitated. They paid little attention to her questions and heatedly debated about her father's going over there to help out.

So she slipped into her room to play the piano. She played very deeply and slowly, one song blending into another. She must have played for a long time for when she was finished the rocker was ominously still. When she left the room, she was frightened to see the lights on and the windows dark. It was evening. She heard the agitated voices talking about her. There were her father, her mother, and Hilda standing in the kitchen, talking nervously. Hilda saw her first. "There she is."

"Well, welcome back," her father said, picking her up with a rough sweep of his arms. She put her hands behind her back as if caught with missing candy. Where have you been all this time, or maybe I should say, this time?"

She looked to Hilda, hoping for the list, but it was not forthcoming. Hilda assumed a firm stance, her arms folded across her large chest, her lips tightly closed. Margaret sighed and drew her hands in front of her. She opened them and looked at the empty palms.

"In my room." She could go that far and still retreat. The expressions on the three faces warned her to retreat.

"We know that is a lie," her father said, the reply prepared long before. "We looked into your bedroom in every corner and you were not there. Now tell me where you were, immediately. You'll be in very big trouble if you don't."

"I was in the cellar."

"You never go in the cellar."

"I did just now. I heard a cat down there so I went down to look."

She watched their faces. Hilda was frustrated. She hadn't checked the cellar. Her parents were not convinced and deeply regretted not having taken a look in the cellar. They could not call her a liar even though they were sure she was one. From that day she limited the number and the duration of her visits.

That fall the family attended the annual covered dish supper at the Methodist Church. Margaret ate and then played with her friends until she grew bored. When the social room at the rear of the church had cleared out, she crept in and sat down at the piano. She played all her favorite songs, and she played the doll's wedding song twice, once in the beginning and once at the end. When she finished she sat quietly at the keyboard, looking at the silent keys.

She screamed when she felt two hands grab her shoulders. Trembling, she turned to the embrace of Evelyn Enders, the church organist. Behind Evelyn stood her mother and father and a couple of other people. They clapped, smiled and congratulated her.

"That was quite a nice piece of music that our young virtuoso played," Evelyn began. "I never heard those songs before. Very nice, very pretty."

"Oh, I make them up."

"She plays at her friend's house. She's been taking lessons there too," her father said. "But I must say, I've never heard her play those songs."

"You should be very proud of your talented daughter," Evelyn said with a smile.

"Oh, them," she said turning back to the piano. "They just keep yelling at me and accusing me of hiding. They aren't proud of me at all."

Her mother rushed over to her and hugged her from behind. Nearly crying she said, "Margaret, that's not true. We're very proud of you, of all the good things you do. We are very impressed with your music. Very impressed."

Margaret was unresponsive. She was waiting for her father do his part.

"I think Margaret will be a good piano player someday, don't you think Evelyn?" he said. "She has talent, I'd say. Do you think she's old enough to take two lessons a week? Would you take her as a pupil?"

Margaret hit the keyboard, stood up, and ran off. No, not lessons from the church organist. Please.

About three weeks later her father left and went to fight in the war. Margaret waited and waited but he did not come back.

One day about ten months after his leaving, Margaret's mother explained that her father was dead. This simply meant that she would never see him again. She had already gotten used to living without him. To continue would not be very difficult. After the church service in his honor she asked her mother if she too would die.

"We will all die," her mother said without emotion. "But it will be a long time, a very long time before you do. I wouldn't worry about it. Not right now anyway."

After her father's death, Margaret's mother grew protective, and Margaret chaffed under the new restrictions.

Her mother explained that she did it out of love. That explanation didn't make it easier for Margaret to endure the strict conditions. Sometimes doors were locked with chains placed near the top, out of her reach unless she got up on a chair. If Margaret wandered too near the edge of the property, she would be summoned either by Hilda or her mother. Hilda would walk her to school and meet her at the end of the day.

The few times she went to play with other children, she noticed that the mothers would not leave them alone, and often her mother would come early to pick her up.

About four months after her father's funeral, Hilda appeared in the hallway, a suitcase in one hand, a large bag in the other. She wore an enormous feathery hat. Her eyes were red and baleful. Her movements were more clumsy and sluggish than normal.

She kissed Margaret on the cheek, said good bye to her mother, did a few pointless movements to the left and to the right, then a complete turn. She lumbered out the door.

Margaret laughed. Hilda reminded her of a dancing bear.

"I wouldn't laugh at poor Hilda," her mother said when Hilda reached the street. "You know how much she loved you." Then wistfully looking at the ceiling, "Poor woman. Just couldn't stand bringing up a girl who keeps disappearing. Margaret was shocked but found out a few days later by listening in on a conversation that her mother simply could not pay Hilda. The money had run out. The piano practices at her friend's house were over. Some months later, they sold the house and moved to an apartment near downtown.

* * *

Margaret walked cautiously up the snow-covered steps, holding the black iron railing for support. She knocked on the door several times, but with her gloved hand she produced almost no sound. She removed the glove and rapped again with her bare knuckles. The white mist of her breath blurred her vision of the door.

Apparently no one was home. Looking back, she saw that hers were the only footsteps in the morning snow. She studied the positions of footprints from the road to the porch but could detect nothing that would indicate the age of their maker. They did not reveal how slowly she walked, how fearful she was of falling. The footprints could have been made by a child. She smiled at that thought and turned back to the door. It was locked.

She went around the back, as she so often had, by way of a driveway that led past the house to a wooden garage near the rear of the property. Even before she reached the backyard, she realized that something was wrong. The maple tree was gone. She was disappointed because it was so prominent in her view through the window. From the middle of the backyard where the tree had been she faced the house and was confused by what she saw. To her left was the kitchen door, then a window that she remembered clearly to be the dining room. There was no window where her room was.

Most surprising was a small protrusion of the wall, about a foot deep, that ran from ground level up to the roof. The roof was extended the necessary foot to accommodate it. She thought of a chimney taking fire from the cellar, racing it up the flue, and spewing it out to the sky. She felt that something was boarded up in that tiny space. A vague fear flooded into her mind. Her skin prickled and her muscles went tense. She felt a horror worse than waking in the dark or watching a scary movie.

She made her way to the back door, which opened to the kitchen, hot tears streaking her face. Had the years deceived her? Were childhood memories taunting her? The backdoor was open and she went into the kitchen. It had been remodeled in a horrible manner. The bright red ceiling had been painted off-white. She walked through the door of the kitchen that led through a short hallway to the dining room. This is where her room should have been. She stood sideways in the hallway and looked ahead past the left side of the staircase. There, just past the closet that was fitted under the staircase, was the trapezoid door that was too small to go through standing up. It was ajar.

She stepped to the right until she reached the kitchen door. She faced the right side of the staircase and the adjoining wall. She moved another step and entered the kitchen. Now she faced the kitchen window. In that case, if she had entered her room and walked the distance to the piano, she would really have passed through the staircase and into the kitchen. Her room was no wider than the staircase. It was uncomfortably short too. Perhaps it too had been remodeled, or there never was a room.

She was overcome with remorse. Her final mission was a failure, her fantasies, folly. She walked beyond the staircase and looked at the trapezoid door. A yellow light glowed within. She bent her knees to the floor and painfully crawled through the door.

The room was exactly as she had left it. The long years of abandonment left no dust on the furniture. The ceramic doll looked steadily at her, and Margaret wept from the deepest part of her soul. A yellow wedge of sunlight lay on the rug and floor. She walked across it to the other side of the room. She touched the rocker. It sprang to life with a movement surprisingly great, and it imparted its life to the room.

The peculiar chess game was on the table by the adjacent wall. Even at a distance she could see that the pieces had not been moved. Neither player had won nor lost.

She looked at the black and white keys of the piano, and slowly she reached out her hand to play a chord. The music leaped into the silence and filled the room. Every piece of furniture reverberated with the chords. She played a few more meaningless chords with useless fingers, and then looked into the deep brown mahogany of the piano, finished like glass. She was looking at a very old woman. A red scarf was about her neck. Her eyes were red and sunken. All across her image ran the dark grains of mahogany.

She left the piano, walked to the center of the room, and stood on the oriental rug. Carefully she sat down, her stiff legs bending slowly and still with pain from crawling through the door. There she sat, looking out the window for hours, maybe days. She saw the green tree on green grass, golden leaves falling from gray branches and resting lightly on the ground. She saw winter hiding the richness of roses. She saw the bare tree, the new grass, the golden leaves, the snow.

DAD'S DUMP

The beer cans I sometimes see in the ditch below my house were not tossed there by some litterbug. They are old—faded, dented and dirty. They have the puncture of the old church key can openers. Some of the brands are gone or hard to find these days—Grand Union, Old Milwaukee. Despite their weathered appearance, they have a familiar look. A few emerge each spring with the rains. They wash down a little stream below my house and into the ditch in front of a neighbor's property. If not picked up, they eventually wash into the creek. If they float, they may end up in the Mohawk River.

It's been more than three years since I have returned to the home where I grew up in Upstate New York. The house is full of my parents' memorabilia—items of transition, accomplishment, recognition—the things they would want people to remember after they are gone. My father's toy sailboat, Gibraltar, won a race in Rochester, New York, when he was 6. There's my father's Coast Guard dress uniform and a thank you letter from President Harry Truman for serving in World War II. My father, a music teacher for 30 years, wrote on a photograph of his 1961 high school band "A in grade 4" at All State competition. On and on, box after box. A wedding picture—1939. My young parents seemed a model of harmony. My mother looks mildly submissive, but she wasn't.

Even as a child, I knew that my mother held the power in the family. I didn't understand at the time how she did that until after my father died. Then I saw how she would hammer and hammer on me relentlessly until I agreed to do whatever she wanted done. That's what she did with my father. Her father was an alcoholic, and so she had an aversion to alcohol. She did not approve of my father's drinking, although in the interest of harmony she tolerated small amounts. Heaven help him if she caught him drinking more than a few beers in a day. So he'd have a public beer, then go outside to check the weather, or maybe he heard a fox by the chicken coop, or the car needed to be moved before the snow storm. He'd come back a while later. Everything was just fine. He'd have another beer and call it quits for the night. My mother would nod approvingly. Two beers in a day never hurt anybody.

When I moved back into the house more than three years ago, my brother told me about a secret beer-can dump where my father threw the cans he did not want to acknowledge drinking. It is in a small gully with a seasonal stream that flows through the adjacent property. The dump was abandoned in the early 1980s, when the New York State bottle deposit bill went into effect and my father decided to abstain from alcohol.

He was occupied with other endeavors back then. One was the eradication of burdocks and other dense weeds that had taken over parts of the property. He fought hard and won a few battles. But as he got older, it was clear he was losing the war. However, in a way he couldn't understand then, the burdocks may have been more friend than foe. Recently I went looking for the beer-can dump, but the burdocks and undergrowth had formed a fortress around the area that seemed intent on preserving the secret. I still haven't found the dump, but I know it is there and I know why it is there. I doubt he ever thought it would be part of his legacy.

But each spring, the rains float a few more cans into the ditch below my house, and I see them on my morning walks. Sometimes I pick them and recycle them. Sometimes I wonder, how long will this go on?

Originally published in the Albany Times Union's Viewpoint, October 25, 2015.

ABOUT THE AUTHOR

Larry Schnell is a writer and journalist living in Van Hornesville near Cooperstown, New York. His first published work, *Laura*, begins the stories set in rural Upstate New York. As a reporter for the Gainesville Sun and the Florida Times-Union in Florida, he covered business, politics, criminal justice, and higher education for eight years. He graduated from the State University of New York at Oneonta with bachelor's degree in English literature and from the University of Florida with a master's in mass communication. He has taught English, journalism and writing for several colleges and the University of Florida. A lifelong sailor and licensed boat captain, he has sailed in Florida, the East Coast, the Bahamas, and Lake Ontario in his sailboat Intrada, and has published articles in boating magazines about his sailing experiences.

Larry Schnell can be reached at larryschnellfl@yahoo.com

Made in the USA
Charleston, SC
09 July 2016